FIRST WEEK FREE

AT THE

ROOMY TOILET

FIRST WEEK FREE

AT THE

ROOMY TOILET

A JUNE KNIGHT MYSTERY

JOSH PACHTER

Contents

Praise for First Week Free at the Roomy Toilet   ii

Prologue: May 31   1

June's Log: June 1   4

June's Log: June 2   15

June's Log: June 3   36

June's Log: June 4   57

June's Log: June 5   80

June's Log: June 6   106

June's Log: June 7   125

Epilogue: May 31 (One Year Later)   153

About the Author   157

Also by Josh Pachter   158

Praise for First Week Free at the Roomy Toilet

"Josh Pachter's *First Week Free at the Roomy Toilet* grabs you from the first page with a witty voice, snappy pace, and June's fun character. The mystery is solid yet unexpected, with twists that keep the reader and June on her toes. As a spokesperson for Yummy Nibbles (dog food), June's perspective and character bring a fresh angle to the young reader book space. Young mystery readers will love the mystery, quirky residents in the Roomy Toilet, and June, who inhabits the adult world in a fun way."—Fleur Bradley, Anthony- and Agatha-nominated author of *Midnight at the Barclay Hotel* and *Daybreak on Raven Island*

"From the brilliantly absurd (or perhaps just absurdly brilliant) mind of Josh Pachter comes a fantastic middle-grade-to-low-YA debut, *First Week Free at the Roomy Toilet.* Filled with winks, nods, and clever wordplay, *First Week Free* had me grinning ear-to-ear from start to an ending chock full of twists and turns I never saw coming."—KB Jackson, Agatha-winning author of the Sasquatch Hunters series

"This was an enjoyable book that I could not put down, quickly becoming a page-turner as I had to know how it was going to end. The mystery was nicely executed, with bits and pieces here and there and a few twists and turns to keep this reader engaged throughout. With visually descriptive narrative and engaging dialogue, the story put me in the middle of the action—and when I thought I had it all figured out, events cascaded with surprises that enhanced my reading pleasure. Overall, a delightfully charming entree into the middle-grade-to-low-YA arena."—Dru Ann Love, *dru's book musings*

"A charming book that can be enjoyed by both adults and younger readers."—Grace Topping, author of the Laura Bishop series

Prologue: May 31

The judge must have been on drugs. That's the only explanation I can think of that makes a lick of sense.

When Morty, my bald agent, first suggested I sue my parents for emancipation, I figured *he* must be on drugs.

"Morty, are you on drugs?" I demanded. "Okay, sure, I look like a stick with blond hair, but I'm not *emancipated*—and, even if I *was*, it's not Mom and Pops' fault. I just don't get hungry much, that's all."

"That's *emaciated*," Morty explained patiently, his twinkling deep-blue eyes a splash of youth in his sixty-year-old face. "I'm talking *emancipated*, Chickie. It's a different situation altogether."

My name is June, not Chickie, but Morty has called me Chickie since the day he began representing me, when I was six. I have no idea where the nickname came from, and I hate it—but Morty is Morty, and he insists.

"Then what's *emancipated*?"

He smiled. "It's a legal term, dolling. It means you become officially an adult, and—"

"An adult? At fourteen? You *are* on drugs."

"Only Pepto Bismol," Morty said, patting his belly with a grimace. Although he drives a snazzy new car and always seems to have plenty of money, Morty could definitely use a woman's hand to help him pick out his clothes. I think he must buy his suits pre-rumpled, and they're always about three sizes too big for him. "About the emancipation, Chickie, I'm poifeckly serious."

"Morty," I acknowledged, "this is certainly a novel idea."

He beamed.

"I'm not sure it's a novel I really want to *read*, though. I mean, why would I want to sue my parents? I *love* my parents!"

"Love, schmove, I'm talking business, dolling. Just think of the publicity! Think of the headlines: 'Fourteen-Year-Old Ectress Takes Parents to Court.'"

"Actress?" I shook my head. "I make thirty-second commercials for dog food."

"The director *makes* them, Chickie. You *ect* in them. This makes you, you should excuse an old man for disagreeing with a know-it-all teenybopper, an ectress."

"All right, fine, I'm an actress. But—"

"I'm not interested in your 'but,'" Morty cut me off—then cut himself off with a lascivious grin. "In ten more years, maybe, if I shouldn't be blind by then. Today, though, I'm more interested in your career. For which a couple nice headlines, let's face it, would do wonders."

He had a point. After eight years as the spokeskid for Yummy Nibbles, the dog food dogs love better than people love people food, I was nearing the end of my current contract extension and beginning to worry that the company was ready to move its advertising in a new— and me-free—direction. And, let's face it, other offers were not exactly pouring in.

"You keep telling me you want to broaden your horizons, Chickie, get out of commercials and into 'real' ecting. But kid ectors are a dime a dozen, dolling, you need to do something special if you want to attract the kind of high-powered attention that'll help you take the next step. Trust me, Chickie. Have I ever steered you wrong?"

I considered the question—and realized that, in fact, Morty's advice over the course of the eight years he'd been representing me had, for the most part, turned out to be sound.

"Okay," I decided, "let's go for it."

The hardest part was convincing Mom and Pops that this wasn't the worst idea in the entire history of human thought. Actually, Morty didn't even want to tell them it was all just a big publicity stunt, but I insisted. No *way* was I going to let them think I was seriously trying to break away from them! It took two full days of argument to win them over, but they'd always been supportive of my career, and they eventually—grudgingly—agreed to go along with the scheme. So then we had to find lawyers for each of us who would play along, and schedule a hearing…

… and, finally, on Thursday, May 31, we spent the afternoon in a stifling courtroom, mostly with me perched on the witness stand emoting. I didn't say one bad word about my parents, but I calmly explained that I was making a pretty decent living doing commercials and was truly ready to be independent and responsible for my own well-being. The part about making a living was an exaggeration, and the part about being ready to be responsible for myself was a flat-out lie, but Morty had written my lines for me, and, if I say so myself, this was the finest performance I'd ever given.

I wrapped up my testimony on the stroke of five, and the judge ordered us to return at two the next afternoon to hear his decision.

The four of us—Mom, Pops, Morty, and me—went out for pizza that night. "What's going to happen tomorrow?" my mother wanted to know.

"Don't worry, sweetheart," Morty reassured her, reaching across the table to pat her hand on his way towards another slice. "Trust me, everything's under control. Efter all, what could possibly go wrong?"

June's Log: June 1

"All rise!" the uniformed bailiff intoned at precisely two in the afternoon.

I stood. Morty stood. My lawyer stood. On the other side of the aisle, Mom and Pops and *their* lawyer all stood. I looked around the courtroom for the press, but, except for us, the cavernous wood-paneled room was empty.

I tugged on Morty's sleeve, and he leaned over and put his ear next to my mouth.

"Where are the reporters?" I whispered.

Before he could reply, an oak door behind the tall mahogany bench creaked open, and the judge grumbled in, his long black robe swirling around him. He carried three thick manila file folders crammed full of documents and settled himself noisily in his chair.

"Fifth Circuit Court is now in session," the bailiff went on. "The Honorable Justice Isidore Blynde presiding. You may be seated."

We all sat down.

Judge Blynde spread the folders out before him, opened one of them, and studied the top page carefully. He closed the folder, opened a second one, shuffled through its contents, selected a page, and read it from top to bottom.

My mom sniffed loudly, and my father handed her a handkerchief. Apparently, I wasn't the only one in the family with a flair for dramatics.

The judge closed the second folder and opened a third one.

Except for my mother's sniffling, the courtroom was silent.

Finally, Judge Blynde closed the third folder, peered at us over the tops of his wire-rimmed spectacles, and cleared his throat.

"I have heard no evidence whatsoever that Mr. and Mrs. Knight are anything other than good and loving parents," he said gruffly. "There have been no accusations of abuse, either physical or emotional. No psychological testimony has been presented."

I knew, of course, that our appearance in court was a scam, a stunt, yet my heart sank when I heard the judge say those words. He hadn't bought it, and he was sending me back home and my career back to Square One. I looked glumly at Morty, who tapped the middle knuckle of his index finger against his pursed lips in a gesture I took to mean *Don't freak out, Chickie. Let the man finish.*

"However," Judge Blynde continued, looking straight at me, "you seem to be a mature young lady who knows what she wants, Ms. Knight, and this court believes that, in the absence of compelling argument to the contrary, it is generally a good idea to allow citizens to make their own decisions."

I wasn't sure I understood all of that, but it seemed to be positive. I perked up, and out of the corner of my eye, I saw the hint of a smile flicker across Morty's face.

"This is, perhaps, an unorthodox ruling, but I'm going to give you a month on your own, Ms. Knight, and we'll see how you like it. We'll reconvene here on"—he paged through a calendar on his desk and made a note—"on Monday, July 2, at 9 AM, and decide whether to make this order permanent or rescind it. For now, though, your motion is temporarily granted, pending further review in one month's time." He banged his gavel loudly on his desktop. "We stand adjourned."

He rose from his chair and went back out through his private door. Even though there weren't any reporters present, my mom did as Morty had coached her and pretended to burst into tears, and Pops pretended to comfort her, threw me a wink, and led her out the back of the courtroom, their attorney scurrying along beside them.

I tugged on Morty's sleeve. "Did we win?" I said.

He leaned down and pinched my cheek like a proud grandma. "We got eggzackly what we wanted, dolling."

"So, can I go home now?"

"Home?" He looked scandalized. "Of course not! You go home, Chickie, and the newspapers will know this whole thing was a gag. You've got to stay as far away from home as you can get."

I guess I hadn't thought very far ahead. "So," I said, my voice small, "what do I do now?"

He took a long white envelope from the inside pocket of his gray suit coat and handed it to me. "You got yourself an ecting job, Chickie," he said. "For the next month, you gotta ect like a grownup."

"But—but where am I supposed to *go*?"

"Look in the envelope, dolling. Everything you need is there. I'd run you over myself, but I got an appointment in the other direction in"—he glanced at his watch—"oy, in twenty minutes! I gotta fly, Chickie, sorry. Call me tonight when you get yourself settled."

He patted me on the head encouragingly, linked arms with my attorney—who I think was his second cousin or something—and the two of them hurried off and left me alone.

Settled? Settled *where*? Settled *how*?

I looked around the courtroom. It was empty. If this was such a hot publicity stunt, where were the paparazzi?

Fourteen-Year-Old Actress Takes Parents to Court, right.

More like *Fourteen-Year-Old Scaredy Cat Has No Clue What to Do Next*.

I opened Morty's envelope and slid out its contents: a single sheet of notepaper wrapped around five crisp twenty-dollar bills.

I unfolded the note and read it.

Congratulations, Chickie, you're emancipated! Try Smedley Street.
xoxo,
Morty the Agent

I'm sure Morty must have a last name, but somehow, I had never learned it. To me, he was always just Morty the Agent.

I looked down at the thin sheaf of bills he'd given me and saw Andrew Jackson gazing soberly past my right shoulder, completely ignoring me.

Congratulations, I thought. Now, why did I feel like "condolences" would have been a more appropriate word choice?

Following Morty's instructions, I left the courthouse—with nothing but the hundred dollars he'd fronted me, a couple of dollars of my own, the dress clothes I'd worn to court, and my backpack—asked directions to Smedley Street and wound my way through the center of town, past cafés and clothing stores, bars and restaurants, the new three-screen movie palace and the old-fashioned ice-cream parlor where Mom and Pops took me for a hot-fudge sundae after every favorable report card. As I passed Aunt Teak's and Uncle Junque's, my father's shop, I thought about trying the door to see if Pops had gone in to work, but Morty had warned me that I might not know it when the press began stalking me, so I clenched my jaw and breezed right on by without slowing my stride.

I finally left downtown behind me and plunged into a maze of residential streets. And, after what felt like an eternity, at last, I turned off Chatman Drive into Smedley Street, a tree-shaded neighborhood lined on both sides with majestic Victorian homes in sedate colors, each perched primly in the center of a rectangle of perfectly manicured lawn.

I'd been walking for almost an hour, and I suddenly realized that I totally had to find a bathroom. As if on cue, I spotted a sign nailed to the trunk of a huge willow tree on the decidedly *un*manicured front yard of a vibrantly purple gingerbread house that seemed completely out of place amongst its neighbors.

ROOMY TOILET, the sign announced, and I let out a breath I hadn't realized I was holding.

I quick-marched up the brick walkway, mounted the five wooden steps to the porch, and pressed the buzzer beside the canary-yellow door.

Somewhere inside the house, a doorbell bonged loudly.

I jiggled up and down on the porch for almost a minute, trying to take my mind off my dilemma by naming the flowers and bushes in the pretty little garden plots on either side of the porch steps—azaleas, rhododendrons, irises, white and mauve wisteria, poppies, pansies, primroses, others I didn't know—and was about to hit the buzzer again when the door swung open, revealing a lady in black Capri pants and a tight hot-pink blouse, bleached blond hair teased up in a beehive that didn't hide her dark roots, brown eyes bright behind a pair of cat-eye glasses with rhinestones studded along the front and sides of the lilac frame, big dangly metal earrings that tinkled with her every movement. The clothes and hair and gaudy costume jewelry made her look like the mom on a black-and-white Nick at Nite sitcom, but underneath her carelessly applied makeup was a woman in her sixties pretending to be young enough to be her own daughter.

"Yeeees?" she drawled, looking me up and down with interest.

"Can I use your bathroom?" I said, bouncing anxiously.

"Excuse me?"

"Your bathroom," I repeated, swiveling my head to glance back at the sign on the tree. "The roomy toilet?"

She blinked at me, uncomprehending—and then she realized what I was saying and made a noise of disgust. "Not *again*," she said. "I swear, I'm going to *strangle* those little monsters." Then, thank goodness, she noticed my predicament and said, "Oh, fine, dear, you go right ahead. It's through the French doors, there, then through the archway and first door on the right."

I bolted past her, zipped through the French doors and across the dining room and under the arch, and found the bathroom—which was actually fairly cramped, not roomy at *all*—and did what I had to do.

By the time I got back to the foyer, the old lady was out on her overgrown lawn, pulling the sign down from the willow and muttering under her breath.

"That's the third time this week," she complained. "I put it up, and those little brats sneak over here when I'm not looking and change it. If I could just get my hands on—"

"What's it *supposed* to say?"

"Room To Let," she said. "This is a boarding house, dear, and I—"

"You rent rooms?"

"Yes, dear, very nice furnished rooms, breakfast and supper and use of the parlor included. Why, do you know someone who's looking for—?"

"*I am!*" I shouted. "*I'm* looking for a room!"

"You? You're just a child!"

"I'm emancipated," I said proudly.

Her eyes narrowed. "You're certainly on the scrawny side, but I wouldn't say *emancipated*."

I sighed. "Never mind," I said. "The point is, I'm looking for a place to stay, Miss—?"

"Mrs.," she corrected me. "Mrs. Prunella Smedleigh."

I did a double-take. "Mrs. Smedley? Are you named after the street, or is the street named after you?"

"Neither, dear. It's S-M-E-D-L-E-I-G-H. And, anyway, that's my poor good-for-nothing second husband's name, not mine."

"I'm sorry, I didn't realize—"

"Oh, no need to apologize, dear. Smedleigh's not dead—just poor. That's why I threw him out. I got tired of his get-rich-quick schemes, none of which ever made him an honest nickel. I never even got a honeymoon out of that man."

"What was your name before you married him?"

"Well, before I married Smedleigh, I was Prunella Smedlee—that's S-M-E-D-L-E-E, from my first husband, Horace Smedlee. Now, *he's* dead, but there's no need to be sorry about that, either. I never much cared for Horace. He was stinking rich, though, and he left me every dime. That's how I was able to afford this place. Smedleigh, the poor man, was one of my very first boarders, but he couldn't afford the rent. He was always a day late and a dollar short—at *least* a dollar, usually more—and I finally decided I had to either evict him or marry him. I didn't have the heart to throw him out, so I became Mrs. Smedleigh and moved him in with me."

"What happened?"

"Turned out the poor man was a better boarder than a husband, so I evicted him, after all. The only thing I kept was his name."

"And what was your name *originally*?"

"Well, I was born Prunella Smeddlea—that's S-M-E-D-D-L-E-A—such an *awful* name. Perhaps that's why I married so young. That and Horace's money, of course."

Fifteen minutes later, Mrs. Smedleigh and I were camped on two of the overstuffed armchairs in her cozy parlor. She was wearing an old-fashioned apron now, decorated with colorful drawings of lemons and cherries, avocados and radishes, scallions and bright-red lobsters, and she'd made us a pot of jasmine tea and set out a plate of Oreos.

Well, not exactly Oreos. The plate was overflowing with dozens of chocolate cookies, but they'd been pulled apart, and the cream filling was gone. As I reached for one, a gorgeous Siamese cat ambled insouciantly into the room and wrapped itself around Mrs. Smedleigh's leg.

"Ah, *there* you are, you little angel," she said. "June, this is Fido."

"Fido?" I said. "That's a dog's name."

"I always wanted a dog," she said wistfully.

"Then why did you get a cat?"

"I'm allergic to dogs." She reached into the oversized pocket on the front of her apron and pulled out a complete Oreo, twisted the two cookies in opposite directions, and held the half with the cream on it out to the cat.

With a happy purr, Fido licked the cream from the cookie, whisked his tail, and strolled off.

Mrs. Smedleigh neatly added the two dark-brown circles to the plate, then held it out to me.

"Cookie?" she said.

"Ah, no, thanks. I—um, I'm not supposed to eat between meals."

"Well," she nodded, "that explains why you're so emancipated."

I shook that one off. "About the room, Mrs. Smedleigh?"

"The room, yes. Well, you're in luck, young lady. I have one room vacant at the moment. It's on the third floor, very nice, twin bed, dresser, wardrobe, very clean. The rent is a hundred and fifty dollars a week."

My heart sank. "That's a little out of my price range," I said. "You haven't got anything cheaper?"

She studied me closely, then held the cookie plate out to me again. "Are you sure you won't have one?"

She was testing me, I realized, and this was a test I needed to pass. At least it was a multiple-choice exam. I usually do pretty well on those.

Hmm. Since Fido only seemed to eat the cream fillings and Mrs. Smedleigh was apparently an expert Oreo separator, I figured I had a fifty/fifty chance.

I selected the cookie that seemed least dripping with cat drool, crammed it into my mouth, and washed it down with a sip from my delicate china cup.

"This is delicious," I said, adding "tea" under my breath.

Mrs. Smedleigh smiled approvingly. "I don't usually rent out the attic room," she said, "since there's no bathroom up there. But I suppose I could let you have it for a hundred a week, including breakfast and supper and use of the parlor. My ladies and gentlemen mostly eat lunch in town, but you may keep a few things in the kitchen, if you'd prefer to make your own."

I thought about the five twenty-dollar bills in my pocket. The money I earned making commercials went straight into a college fund, where I couldn't touch it, so Morty's hundred and the forty-odd dollars in my personal savings account at the Mercantile Bank in town were all the ready cash I had in the world.

"If you sign a three-month lease," the landlady added, "your first week is free. That's the policy of the house. After that, you pay one week at a time on the first day of each following week."

A three-month lease? According to Morty, I'd get all the publicity I needed in *one* month. Then, on July 2, I could tell the judge I'd changed my mind and go home.

How was I supposed to come up with enough money to make it through a month on my own, though?

A free first week and a second week I could afford to pay for with Morty's money would give me time to figure out how to make the rest of the lease period work. Maybe my agent could advance me something against my next paycheck from Yummy Nibbles. Mom and Pops wouldn't approve of my diverting that money away from my college account—but, hey, what was the good of being emancipated if I couldn't start making my own financial decisions?

"I'll take it," I decided.

Mrs. Smedleigh fetched a simple, one-page lease agreement from the rolltop desk in the corner of the parlor, and I filled in my name—June

Knight—at the top and signed and dated the blank line at the bottom.

"Lovely," she smiled. "Now, you just sit right there and enjoy your tea for a few moments, and I'll run up and make the bed and leave fresh towels in the bottom dresser drawer. Supper is at six-thirty. Tonight I am serving chicken cordon blue. You'll like it."

"Does, um, does Fido help with the cooking?" I asked.

She shook her head. "Just with the cookies."

That was a relief.

And she topped off my cup, filed the signed lease in one of the rolltop's drawers, and bustled away up the stairs.

The house was very quiet. I sipped my tea and listened to the silence and let my mind drift back over the events of the day.

Were we doing the right thing? The more I thought about it, the more harebrained our scheme seemed. And, for a publicity stunt, it certainly hadn't attracted any actual publicity.

Not yet, I reminded myself. Morty had warned us it might take a day or two before the papers got wind of the story.

Trust Morty, a voice inside my head whispered softly. *Morty knows best. Trust Morty....*

"You're all set, dear," Mrs. Smedleigh said brightly, and my eyes popped open. Had I fallen asleep? "Would you like me to show you the room?"

"No, that's all right," I said, yawning. "I'll find it."

"Supper at six-thirty, then?"

"It's been kind of a long day, Mrs. Smedleigh. I may just skip supper tonight. Do you mind?"

"Not at all, dear. You just see how you feel. There'll be plenty of food, if you change your mind, and everyone will be looking forward to meeting you. Otherwise, *le petit dejeuner* is at seven-thirty on weekdays, at nine on Saturdays and Sundays. That's French, dear, for breakfast."

I thanked her, struggled up from the comfortable armchair, climbed two flights of carpeted stairs to the third floor, and then a narrow uncarpeted third flight to the attic.

My new room was small and simple: yellow wallpaper with little pink flowers all over it, hardwood floor, a four-poster bed with a yellow comforter peppered with tiny red dots, a plain deal bedside table with a lamp and a windup alarm clock, an old pine dresser painted pale green, a La-Z-Boy recliner with worn tan upholstery, a cracked porcelain sink beneath a mirrored medicine cabinet in the corner, one little window with yellow curtains drawn across it that looked down across the unkempt front yard to peaceful Smedley Street. The furniture was old, and the colors of the chair and the dresser didn't match the bright yellows of the walls and bed and curtains, but everything seemed clean and well cared for.

I called Mom and Pops on my cell phone to tell them where I was. Mom cried a little, and Pops offered to drive right over with my pjs and toothbrush and Bennington, the teddy bear I've had since before I was born, but I told him I'd come by tomorrow morning to pick up a suitcase.

"It's no trouble, Junie," he said, and there was a catch in his voice that told me how troubled *he* was feeling about the whole crazy situation.

"Thanks, Pops, but I'm really tired. I think I'm just gonna go to bed. I'll see you tomorrow."

There was a silence on the line. Then: "I certainly hope Morty knows what he's doing," Pops said.

"He better," I agreed. "If this doesn't work out, I'm gonna *kill* him."

He forced a chuckle. "You're sure you're okay, Junebug?"

"I'm sure, Pops. I miss you guys already, though. I love you both."

"We love you, too, June. Sleep tight."

I closed my phone and looked around me. I had no pjs, no toothbrush, no book to read, no Bennington.

Without even taking off my court clothes, I collapsed into bed.

June's Log: June 2

I awoke to the distant smell of bacon frying—which told me at once that something wasn't kosher, since bacon does not fry in our house.

We're not Jewish—being Jewish is Morty's department—it's just that my mom is a vegetarian.

Speaking of religion, we are Unitarians. Which, yes, makes me a vegetarian Unitarian.

You think that's bad? Then maybe I shouldn't mention that my dad's birthday is on Groundhog Day, and his shop—as you may have guessed from its name—is an antique store, which makes *him* a vegetarian Unitarian Aquarian antiquarian.

Try saying *that* three times fast.

Anyway, although we don't eat meat at home, I have snuck in the odd cheeseburger while out of the parental orbit, and I know what frying bacon smells like. So it was with some trepidation that I opened my eyes a crack and looked around me.

Yellow wallpaper with little pink flowers all over it. A cracked porcelain sink in the corner.

I had no idea where I was.

I opened my mouth to scream—and suddenly, the day before came rushing back to me.

The courtroom, Judge Blynde, the gavel, Mom's pretend weeping,

Morty's envelope, my long trek across town, the Roomy Toilet….

I was emancipated!

By the time I got down to the dining room, still wearing my court clothes and silver stud earrings from the day before, the other tenants were already seated around the black pedestal lion's-paw table, and the bacon was already almost gone.

Mrs. Smedleigh came in from the kitchen carrying a platter piled high with pancakes. Her face lit up with a smile when she saw me. "Ah, *there* you are, dear! You must be famished." She indicated an empty chair with a nod of her head and said, "This one's yours, dear. Have you met the family? Two pancakes, or three?"

"I just came in," I said, settling into the chair and unfolding a pink cloth napkin across my lap. "One, please."

As if I hadn't spoken, she spatulaed three pancakes onto the plate in front of me and said, "You go ahead and take those last two strips of bacon, dear. Everyone else has had theirs. Now, there's coffee in the thermos, milk in the jug—I buy two percent, dear, I hope that's all right—and orange juice in the pitcher. Just help yourself to whatever you like and sing out if anything runs low. There's more of everything in the kitchen."

I reached for the milk jug and poured myself a glass.

"This is June," the landlady began brightly, then hesitated a moment in confusion. "What *was* your last name again, dear?"

"Knight," I said, spreading margarine onto my pancakes.

"June Knight," she continued. "Isn't that a pretty name?" She laid an extra pancake in front of the elderly gentleman sitting at the head of the table to my right. "And this, dear, is Mr. Le Groth, third floor back. Until you arrived, he was my newest boarder."

"It's *Dr.* Le Groth," the old guy grumbled. He was dressed in a three-piece dark-brown houndstooth suit, white shirt, and wine-red necktie, and his thick head of snowy hair and bushy salt-and-pepper mustache were perfectly trimmed. His dark-brown eyes glared at the landlady fiercely. "I have been living under your roof for almost a month, madam, and I would think that by now, you would do me the courtesy of addressing me with a modicum of professional respect." When Mrs. Smedleigh looked properly abashed, he turned to me. "I am Simeon Le Groth, MD, Miss Knight, and I prefer to be addressed as Dr. Le Groth."

"Good morning, Doctor," I said. I held out my hand, and he shook it quite formally. When he released it, I kept it extended and said, "Um, would you pass the syrup, please?"

"Ah, ahem, of course," he rumbled and handed me a little white porcelain pitcher.

To the doctor's right and directly across from me sat a man in his forties who looked like a leftover from the Sixties. His dirty-blond hair was long and wild, he had a scraggly beard and gold wire-rimmed John Lennon glasses and wore a fringed leather vest over a tie-dyed T-shirt. Around his neck was a string of white cowrie shells.

"This is Andrew Moore," said Mrs. Smedleigh. "Third-floor front."

The aging hippie attacked the pancake she set before him as if he hadn't eaten in a week, then threw down his knife and fork and held up the index and middle fingers of his right hand as if he were ordering two more. "Peace and love, baby," he said with a blurry grin. "And call me Moonchild. 'Andrew' is so, like, *straight*, you know?"

I held up my own right-handed version of a V, made out of my thumb and forefinger, then put a left-handed one beside it and touched the two thumbs together in a W. "Whatever," I said. "Moonchild works just fine for me."

"Would you please keep your feet to yourself, Mr. Montague?" the attractive young woman to my left complained, glaring angrily at the handsome young man sitting across from her and on Moonchild's right.

"I didn't touch you," he protested, pushing back from the table.

"You most certainly *did*," she snapped, "and I do *not* welcome the attention."

They were about the same age, middle twenties. He was clean-cut and clean-shaven with wavy brown hair, dressed in an open-necked orange Polo shirt and neatly pressed khaki cargo pants, and she was a fair-skinned strawberry blonde with gorgeous hazel eyes and blond highlights in her shoulder-length straightened hair and side-swept bangs. She was wearing a tasteful ivory sweater set and cream-colored slacks.

"This is Jeffrey Montague," Mrs. Smedleigh said. "Second floor back, above the kitchen. He—"

"He may be a Montague," the angry young woman interrupted, "but trust me, June, he's no Romeo. He thinks the way to make a girl notice him is to stomp on her feet."

"It wasn't *me*," the young man insisted.

At that moment, an irritated purr sounded from somewhere below, and Fido padded out from beneath the tablecloth, picked his way carefully around the young woman's chair, and stalked haughtily past me through the archway leading back to the kitchen.

The young woman's face turned as pink as my napkin, and she busied herself adding cream and sugar to her coffee cup.

"Next time, try looking under the table before you bite my head off," Jeffrey Montague scowled. "Anyway, I wouldn't touch your foot with a ten-foot Albanian."

"Al—you mean a ten-foot *pole*," I said. "Don't you?"

"Everyone always picks on the Poles," he said. "Can't I pick on somebody else for a change?"

"Mr. Montague's ancestors came to America from Albania," Mrs. Smedleigh explained, setting two more pancakes on his plate to placate him. "The family name was originally Montagescu, isn't that right, Jeffrey?"

"The immigration officer changed it at Ellis Island," he acknowledged. "Pleased to meet you, June. It's about *time* we get a sympathetic young female face to look at while we eat. I'll tell you, the sour pusses on *these* two"—and he nodded grimly in turn at the young woman and the Roomy Toilet's final tenant, a spinsterish woman of Mrs. Smedleigh's age who sat to his right at the foot of the table, in between himself and the young woman—"could curdle the milk."

"I'll thank you to keep your comments to yourself, Mr. Montague," said the spinster primly. She wore a pearl-gray sweater vest over a white cotton blouse buttoned all the way up to her throat and a conservatively tailored dark-gray skirt. Her gray hair was tied back in a tight bun, and the inexpertly applied circles of rouge on her cheeks were the only hints of color about her. A pair of gunmetal wire-rimmed eyeglasses hung from a chain around her neck.

"Miss Roberts," Mrs. Smedleigh introduced her. "Second floor, front. She's a retired schoolteacher from Walla Walla, Oregon."

"Isn't Walla Walla in Washington?" I asked.

"Of course it is," Miss Roberts said with ill-concealed contempt. "Every child learns that in fourth-grade geography." She poured hot water into her cup, unwrapped an Earl Grey teabag from her severe black pocketbook, and dipped it carefully in the water. "Speaking of which, why aren't *you* in school, young lady? It can't possibly be summer vacation yet."

"No, ma'am," I confirmed. "I used to be home-schooled, but now that I'm not living at home anymore, I'm not sure *what's* going to happen."

"Well," she said, dabbing fastidiously at her pale lips with her napkin, "perhaps *I* shall have to take charge of your education. I *am* still certified, despite my retirement."

"Is that certified or certifiable?" Jeffrey Montague asked in an innocent undertone, and Moonchild burst out in a fit of giggles.

"That's quite enough, gentlemen," Dr. Le Groth said sternly. "And I use the term 'gentlemen' loosely."

Mrs. Smedleigh finished her circuit of the dining table, dropping the last of her pancakes on the plate of the angry young woman to my left. "Last but not least," she said, "this is Ms.—"

"Don't tell me *your* name is Capulet," I teased.

"Heaven forbid." She rolled her eyes. "It's Justice, actually. Libby Justice. I'm second-floor back, across the hall from the bathroom and next door to Prince Charming."

"Is it Libby like Elizabeth?"

"No, in fact, it's short for Liberty." She blushed again. "My full name is Liberty N Justice."

"Really? That's so cool! What's the N stand for?"

"Nothing."

"Liberty Nothing Justice? What the—?"

"No, no, it doesn't stand for Nothing. It stands for nothing."

"I—"

"My middle name is N, the letter N," she explained patiently. "Like the S in Harry S Truman. It gets longer when you abbreviate it."

"Another hotcake?" Mrs. Smedleigh offered.

Libby patted her flat stomach and shook her head. "Have to watch my weight," she said brightly.

"I'll take it," said Moonchild. "My weight's all grown up, man—I don't *have* to watch it anymore."

"Libby and I are locals and went to school together," Jeffrey Montague told me helpfully. "When we were in junior high—around your age, probably—she ran for president of the Student Council. Her campaign slogan was 'Liberty N Justice For All.'"

"That's awesome!" I exclaimed. "You must have murdered the other candidates!"

She shook her head furiously. "There was only one other candidate," she muttered through clenched teeth. "And I had acne and a pot belly and wore braces, and Mr. Wonderful here was on the football team and looked like, well, like *that*. He killed me."

"And, as you can see," Jeff grinned, "she's been trying to return the favor ever since."

"*Mister* Montague," Libby said scathingly, "if I told you I find you irresistibly fascinating, would you realize I was lying?"

"Just one big happy family," Mrs. Smedleigh announced ironically. "You'll fit right in, dear, I'm sure!"

After breakfast, I grabbed my backpack from my room and took off for home to pick up some clothes and other stuff. Mrs. Smedleigh, I noticed, had tacked a new ROOM TO LET sign to the trunk of the willow, this time a good two feet higher than the last one.

Approaching Chatman Drive, I saw two small boys in grubby T-shirts and jeans coming towards me. One was about eight and the other maybe six, so the little folding ladder they carried between them was a foot further from the ground on the eight-year-old side than the six-year-old side.

"Hey, I know you!" the taller of the boys announced as I came abreast of them.

"I don't think you do," I said.

"Sure, I do! You're the Yummy Kibbles girl!"

"Nibbles," I said.

He nudged the other boy in the side with an elbow. "Look, Carson, it's the Yummy Kibbles girl!"

Carson nodded solemnly but said nothing.

"Can I have your autograph?" the older boy said. "It's not for me—it's for him. He's your biggest fan."

"Isn't that nice?" I said. I leaned down to the little guy. "You like my commercials?"

"He likes Yummy Kibbles," the older boy announced.

"It's Nibbles," I said.

"Do *not*," Carson said.

"Do, *too*," the older boy snapped. "He eats them all the time. He's a little *daw*-gie."

Carson dropped his end of the ladder and punched the older boy in the arm. "Am *not*, Dylan."

"Are, *too*," Dylan said, "and you love Yummy Kibbles more than people love people food." Then he turned back to me and added, "So can he have your autograph, or what?"

This was a first for me. I'd been recognized once or twice, and a couple of the kids in my *real* neighborhood treated me like a minor celebrity, but this was the first time I'd ever been asked for an autograph.

"I don't have anything to write with," I said.

Dylan dug in a pocket of his jeans and pulled out a Sharpie.

"I don't have anything to write *on*," I said.

"Write on Carson," Dylan suggested. "Carson, let the lady sign your arm."

Carson obediently stuck out his left arm.

"He's a *good* little doggie," Dylan said.

"I'm *not* a doggie. I'm a *boy*!"

"And I'm sure you're a *good* little boy," I said. "Is Dylan a good brother?"

"He's not my brother," Carson said. "He's my *step*brother."

"I see. Well, can we set up that ladder for you to lean your arm on?"

"It's not a ladder," Dylan said. "It's a *step*ladder."

"I see," I said. "That *step*ladder, then."

Dylan and Carson stood the stepladder on its legs, and Carson laid his arm across the topmost step. *To Carson,* I wrote, being careful not to puncture his skin with the broad tip of the Sharpie. *Save the Yummy Nibbles for the dog.* I underlined the N in Nibbles. *Yours, June Knight.*

"Thanks, lady," Carson beamed. "I'll never wash this arm again!"

"You already never wash it," Dylan said.

The two boys hoisted their ladder and set off again down Smedley Street.

It wasn't until later that I thought to wonder where they were going with a stepladder and a Sharpie.

It took me almost an hour to work my way across town to Essington Lane, listening to Ed Sheeran and Billie Eilish and Madonna on my iPhone and keeping my eyes peeled for journalists. By the time I got there—still without spotting a single scribbler or shutterbug lurking in the bushes—I was hot and sweaty and hungry and parched. Pops was at the store, but Mom was in the house and so excited to see me it was hard to believe I'd been gone for less than twenty-four hours.

We gravitated naturally into the kitchen, which in our house has always been the center of activity. I climbed onto one of the barstools that line the breakfast-nook side of our kitchen counter and watched the precision of her movements as she turned getting glasses from the cupboard and the lemonade pitcher from the fridge into a single liquid flow of motion. She's a small woman, barely five-two—I was as tall as she is by the time I turned twelve, and now, at five-five, I practically tower over her. She's thirty-eight years old—four years younger than my father—but, with her blond hair cut boyishly short and her gentle brown eyes and quick smile, she could pass for twenty-eight if it wasn't for her clothes, which I have to admit are sometimes a little old-fashioned. She was looking pretty hip today, though, in a clingy black V-necked sweater over gray pinstriped slacks I'd convinced her to buy, the last time we'd been out to the mall. She poured us each a glass of lemonade and settled down beside me, leaned in to brush the back of her hand across my cheek, and said, "Now, Junie, tell me all about it!"

The lemonade was ice-cold and tart and delicious, and by the time I'd told her all about Mrs. Smedleigh and the Roomy Toilet, gruff Dr. Le

Groth and bickering Libby and Jeff and the spinsterish Miss Roberts and zonked-out Moonchild, our glasses and the pitcher were empty.

"It sounds—great," Mom said, but I knew she didn't really mean it.

"It's okay, I guess. Morty says I only need to stay there for a month, and then I can come home."

She wiped a bit of lemon pulp from the corner of my mouth with a dishtowel. "I hope that man knows what he's doing," she said.

"He's given us good advice *so* far."

While Mom whipped up a bowl of tuna salad—the way I like it, with hard-boiled egg and celery and a little mustard and pickle relish mixed in—I went upstairs to my room to pack.

I put a Brittney Spears CD into my stereo, cranked up the volume, lit a vanilla-scented candle I'd brought home from some long-ago summer vacation, and spun around slowly, drinking in the sights and smells of the cozy room I'd grown up in, reliving past triumphs and tragedies as my gaze touched on some of the trophies I'd collected during my fourteen years on the planet.

There were posters, of course, all over the walls: movie stars and pop singers, reproductions of Edvard Munch's *The Scream* and Picasso's *Hands With Bouquet*, a flag from Siena's caterpillar *contrada* and a Nepalese batik print of Buddha sitting beneath the Bodhi tree. Almost a hundred Beanie Babies left over from when I was a kid peeked out from the shoe holder hanging on the back of my door. A Magic 8-Ball, six Yodas, a small bronze elephant-headed Ganesha, and Funko Pop! figurines of Beetlejuice and Grogu in a Santa hat stood in an orderly row on my desk. A line of circus pennants was tacked to the wall above my folding closet doors, souvenirs from family outings to Barnum & Bailey, the Big Apple Circus, and a magical autumn evening at Cirque du Soleil. In a printer's letterbox from Pops' store was my collection of blue erasers: spaceships, dinosaurs, jungle animals, cars, Popeye characters. My antiques were on a wall shelf: the stereopticon and slides, the Ansco Viking Readyset camera, the Remington 5 typewriter that still *worked*. A dream catcher I made myself from a kit Pops' brother, my Uncle Richard, sent me one Christmas hung from the ceiling. Action figures of John, Paul, George and Ringo in their Sgt. Pepper outfits clustered around a Blue Meanie and a Lego Yellow Submarine. On my bookshelves, Daniel Pinkwater's *Borgel* and Ellen Raskin's *The Westing Game* and Louis Sachar's *Sideways Stories from Wayside School* shared space with a dozen Jessica Fletchers and Agatha Christies and the first six volumes of *The Chronicles of Narnia* (I've read them a dozen times apiece at least, but I decided long ago that I never want to read the last one, because I like knowing that there will always be more to the story)....

As Britney pointed out that—like me—she used to think she had the answers to everything, but now she knows life doesn't always go her way, yeah, I filled a toiletry bag with shampoo and conditioner, toothbrush and toothpaste, deodorant, pink disposable razor and shaving gel. I pulled a wheelie suitcase from my closet, tossed it onto my bed and packed it with jeans, shorts, a skirt, some good shirts and T-shirts, underwear, socks, tennies, flip-flops, a light jacket for cool evenings. I selected half a dozen books I'd been wanting to read or reread and a volume of a hundred Sudoku puzzles I'd barely cracked. I picked three posters and carefully took them down from my walls, rolled them up and slipped a rubber band around them, then added several favorite pairs of earrings, my MacBook, the A/C adapters for the laptop and my cell phone, and, finally, Bennington, my childhood friend.

When I got back down to the kitchen, Mom had sandwiches, carrot sticks, and chips on the counter and was listening to the radio as she stood, her back to me, washing the dishes. She looked so normal, so *ordinary*, standing there at the sink, her pale-green rubber gloves scrubbing away at the morning's pots and pans. The radio was playing her favorite oldies station, something about a green-eyed lady, passion's lady, rolling slowly across the sands, and Mom hummed along with the music—out of key as ever.

I'd seen that exact same sight a hundred times over the years—a *thousand* times, probably—but for some reason, it hit me now in a way it never had before.

She turned around when she heard me sniffle, and she stripped off her gloves and wrapped me in a warm hug that made me feel like I was about four years old and absolutely safe. A whole minute went by like that, and then she laughed one short laugh and broke the clinch, turned down the radio's volume, and joined me at the counter.

We ate our sandwiches and chattered away about nothing in particular, while in the background the oldies gave way to a newscast—the mayor had decided not to run for a third term, there were no leads on the solo bank robber who'd hit a downtown savings and loan for forty thousand dollars in cash yesterday afternoon, an overturned semi had spilled live chickens all over the interstate, a fifty percent chance of rain for the rest of the weekend—then kicked back into musical gear again, with tight harmonies having fun fun fun till their daddy took the T-Bird away.

Much too soon—way before I was ready to go—I realized that it was time.

"Let me run you over there in the car," Mom offered.

"I don't think that's a good idea," I said wistfully. It sounded like a *great* idea to me, much better than rolling my stupid suitcase across town for an hour—but the whole point of the emancipation stunt was to attract the sort of headlines that would help my career, not "Wimpy Nibbles 'Actress' Needs Mommy to Help Cross Street."

Mom pushed a little, and I was glad she tried, but I held firm. We finally compromised: she called me a cab, and I paid for the ride myself out of the hundred dollars Morty had given me. The fare was seven dollars and fifty cents, and I gave the cabbie a twenty and asked for ten dollars back, which left me with an even ninety dollars of Morty's stake, plus the couple of bucks I'd started out with in the first place.

When the taxi dropped me back at Smedley Street, I saw that the new ROOM TO LET sign tacked to the willow tree had been altered to read BROOM CLOSET.

I let out an exasperated sigh, reached up on tiptoe, and tore it down. The hand-printed changes seemed to have been written with a Sharpie. I tucked the sign under my arm and wrestled my suitcase up the porch steps and into the house.

Mrs. Smedleigh was in the foyer, squeegeeing the insides of the tall, narrow windows on either side of the front door.

"The little monsters have done it again," I complained, showing her the sign.

To my surprise, she waved a dismissive hand. "It doesn't signify, dear," she said. "I meant to go out and take the sign down, anyway: I've rented the room!"

"Oh, that's great!" I congratulated her. "Who's the new tenant?"

"Mr. Marlowe, a charming young man. You'll meet him at dinner. I *do* hope you'll be joining us tonight. We're having chicken cordon bleu."

I narrowed my eyes. "Isn't that what you served last night?"

She laughed gaily. "No, no, dear, that was chicken cordon *blue.* Tonight is chicken cordon *bleu*—it's French."

To celebrate filling the Roomy Toilet's last available room, Mrs. Smedleigh had a vase of bright-yellow daffodils, violet forget-me-nots, and white clematis in the center of the dining table. The scents of the fresh-cut flowers blended with the warm aroma of baking chicken wafting out from the kitchen, and the seven of us gathered around the table in a mostly festive mood.

Miss Roberts was a little put out that the decision had been made to squeeze an extra place setting for the new tenant onto her end of the table, between her and Libby Justice, which forced her to move closer to Jeff Montague, but she didn't put up *too* big a fuss—maybe because the newcomer was practically Brad Pitt handsome.

He was a little young for her, though, maybe twenty-three or twenty-four years old.

"This is Philip Marlowe," Mrs. Smedleigh introduced him, then went around the table and said each of our names.

"Miss Roberts, Jeff, Moonchild, Dr. Le Groth, June, and Libby," he repeated without hesitation or error. "And I'm Phil. Delighted to meet you all!"

"Excellent memory, sir," Dr. Le Groth praised him. "Do you use some sort of mnemonic trick to process the new data?"

He shook his head. "I'm just good with names, I guess," he said.

"Back in a jiffy!" Mrs. Smedleigh announced brightly and dashed through the archway that led past the downstairs bathroom to the kitchen.

The more I looked at him—and, trust me, he was easy to look at, with his straight nose and strong chin and wavy brown hair—the more familiar he seemed to me.

"Do I know you from somewhere?" I said at last.

"I don't think so, but *I* know *you*, don't I?"

"Excuse me?"

"I'm good with faces, too. You're the Yummy Nibbles girl. I've seen you on TV."

I could feel my cheeks flush.

"The girl is embarrassed," Dr. Le Groth said. "Perhaps we should change the subject."

"No, it's okay," I said. "I'm just not used to being recognized. By adults, I mean. Kids come up to me all the time. I got asked for my autograph earlier today."

"That's exciting," Libby said.

"It was fun," I agreed. "I—"

But then Mrs. Smedleigh bustled in with a tray piled with serving bowls of vegetables and russet potatoes and a platter of chicken cordon bleu, which turned out not to be blue at *all*. As she arranged everything neatly around the vase in the center of the table, we talked a little about the TV biz and my career.

"Help yourselves, dears," said Mrs. S. Moonchild was already chewing breaded chicken breast stuffed with ham and melty cheese before she disappeared back through the kitchen arch.

"I know Dr. Le Groth's a doctor and Miss Roberts used to be a teacher," I said, spooning sugar snap peas onto my plate. "But what about the rest of you? What do *you* do?"

"Well, I'm a legal secretary," Libby said. "I work for a small law firm in town. They're a great group." She looked down at her plate and added, under her breath, "Mostly."

"And Jeff?"

He set down his knife and fork, planted his elbows on the table, and rested his chin on his interlaced fingers. "I'm an attorney," he drawled, "at a small law firm in town."

Suddenly, they all seemed very busy with their food.

"I'm a salesman," Phil said at last, ending the awkward silence.

"A salesman," I repeated, with more excitement than the statement really called for. "What do you sell?"

"Commodities," he said. "It's kind of complicated, but I—"

"I don't have to work," Moonchild interrupted, his mouth full of chicken. "I'm on disability."

"I don't mean to be rude," Miss Roberts said—rudely, I thought—"but you don't seem disabled to *me*. You seem quite healthy. Muscular."

"There's nothing wrong with me *physically*, man. I've got PTSD."

I turned to Dr. Le Groth for an explanation.

"It—I'm not sure it's something I should be discussing in front of a person of your age, Miss Knight."

"Oh, come on, I'm not a baby. Moonchild, *you* tell me: what's PTSD? Is it like an STD?"

Jeff broke into a fit of laughter, and even the grim Miss Roberts had to force herself to hide a smile.

"No, man," Moonchild shook his head. "It's Post-Traumatic Stress Disorder. I was in the Army, stationed in Syria, helping to keep the oil safe for democracy, you know, and I got sort of, like, shell-shocked. They call it battle fatigue, too, but I never saw any real combat."

"Besides," Jeff whispered, "PTSD reminds him of LSD."

"Shut *up!*" Libby hissed.

"It kind of messed with my head a little, so I'm not really too good with, like, jobs and stuff."

"Anyone need more of anything?" Mrs. Smedleigh asked, re-emerging from her lair at the back of the house.

We all made happy full noises.

"That was delicious," I said. "Just as good as my mom's cooking!"

"Why, *thank* you, dear, what a lovely compliment! Coffee in the parlor, everyone? And perhaps a glass of milk for you, June?"

"Could I have some more of that tea instead? That was really good."

"None for me, thanks." Phil stretched and yawned. "I'm exhausted," he said and glanced at his watch.

"Is that a Rolex?" Libby asked.

"Oyster Professional Explorer," he nodded, holding his wrist out to her. "Isn't it gorgeous? My folks gave it to me when I graduated from college."

It looked like any other wristwatch to me, but from the way Libby was oohing and aahing, I got it that this was something special. She had Phil's wrist in her hands, turning it this way and that to examine the silver band and black numbered face from various angles—and suddenly, I found myself wondering if she was really interested in the watch, or if she was just using it as an excuse to hold hands with him.

"I think I'll turn in," Phil said, gently pulling his arm free and getting to his feet.

"So early?" Libby asked. "It's not even seven-thirty."

"I'm pretty wiped out from moving in," he explained. "I'll see you all in the morning."

I knew how he felt, having done some moving in myself that day, but for some reason, I was full of energy, and, when the rest of them adjourned to the parlor, I went along.

The parlor was the Roomy Toilet's largest and certainly its most comfortable room. There was a plush floral-patterned sofa and five overstuffed armchairs. Heavy woven curtains were drawn across the big picture window in the south wall, which looked out across the porch to the front yard and Smedley Street, and the small window on the west wall, which looked onto the more sedately painted Victorian next door. The walls themselves were an earthy pea-green, and there were framed hunting prints hanging here and there. The rolltop desk where Mrs. Smedley kept her blank and signed leases and other business papers was in the southwest corner (I think my dad had one like it in the store a couple of years ago—maybe that's where Mrs. Smedleigh bought it!), and a low coffee table strewn with magazines in front of the sofa and end tables bearing table lamps on either side of it. The whole north wall was built-in shelving lined with old books in a rainbow of paper dustjackets and *Reader's Digest* three-in-one novels, a stack of boxed board games at the far left, and a lifetime's accumulation of knickknacks and whatnots and geegaws filling the spaces not given over to literature.

Two of the armchairs were arranged to face an old Emerson television in a dark hardwood cabinet, which had been situated in front of the wall of bookshelves, and Dr. Le Groth and Miss Roberts settled into them like an old married couple. These were clearly their regular after-dinner seats: there was a thick leatherbound volume waiting for him on his and a cross-stitched sampler in progress for her on hers, and they picked up where they'd apparently left off last night without a word to each other or anyone else.

Moonchild and I took two of the other trio of chairs, which faced each other in a little conversation nook by the western window, and that left Libby and Jeff on opposite ends of the sofa.

"What was that crack all about?" Jeff said in a low voice, just loud enough to be overheard.

"What crack?"

"You know what crack. 'Mostly.' I'm as nice to you as anyone else in the office, Libby. Nicer."

"Of course you are. You're the nicest man I know, Jeff. That's why I like you so much. Moonchild? June? Swing around this way and join the party, why don't you?"

We did, and Mrs. Smedleigh brought in the coffee and my tea and set the tray on the coffee table between us and the sofa. The conversation was strained, thanks to the obvious tension between Libby and Jeff, but we struggled along for a while.

"This is an awesome house," I tried. "I haven't seen the outside after dark yet, but I bet it's really scary."

"Yeah, it's freaky deaky," Moonchild agreed. "This neighborhood must be a trip on Halloween."

Jeff reached for the coffee pot. "It reminds me of those corny old Gothic novels people used to read, the Had I But Knowns."

"I liked those," Libby said.

"You would."

She ignored him. "Daphne du Maurier, Mary Stewart, Phyllis—"

"They all had the exact same front cover: it's the dead of night, and some sweet young long-haired blonde in a flowing white dress with a look of unspeakable horror on her face is running away from a house like this one with one lamp burning in an attic window."

"That's my room!" I said proudly.

"I never read them," Jeff went on, "but I bet the stories were as cookie-cutter as the covers."

"That's what we need with this coffee, man."

We all turned to Moonchild in surprise.

"A Gothic novel?" I said.

"No, man, *cookies.*" He got heavily to his feet and drifted off toward the kitchen.

"That dope's got Halloween going on between his ears, three hundred and sixty-five days a year," Jeff said.

"Oh, very sensitive. The man got messed up serving his country, Mr. Montague. He's not a dope."

"He's *smoked* enough dope to—"

"Stop it," Libby said quickly, with a surreptitious nod in my direction. "Little pitchers have—"

"It's okay," I said. "I'm fourteen years old, not four—I know what 'dope' is. But I don't think you should be making fun of Moonchild. Whatever made him like this, it wasn't his fault. He can't help the way he is."

"Exactly," Libby nodded.

Jeff held up his hands in surrender. "I apologize," he said. "You're right. That was just *me* being a dope."

Moonchild never came back, with or without cookies, and one by one, the rest of them said their goodnights and headed up to their rooms. By eight-thirty, when Mrs. Smedleigh wafted in to collect the tray and cups and saucers with Fido trailing along at her heels like a little shadow, I was the only one still in the parlor.

"Just turn out the lights when you go to bed, dear," she said and left me alone.

I looked around the empty room and sighed. My new home.

I went over to the TV and searched for a remote, but there wasn't one. There were little knobs on the set itself, though, so I sat cross-legged on the rust-colored shag carpet and turned it on and flipped through the channels. There were only five of them—the Roomy Toilet had no cable!—and there wasn't anything good on. I turned the set off and stood up.

Dr. Le Groth's leather tome lay on his chair where he'd left it. I guess I'd just assumed it was a medical book, but, now that I saw it close up, I was able to read the title and author's name stamped in gold leaf on the front cover: *Swifty: My Life and Good Times*, by Irving Lazar. It looked pretty boring, and I didn't even bother to open it.

Miss Roberts' cross-stitch project was face up on *her* chair. Centered across the inside of two gray stone tablets were the number 8 and the words: "Thou Shalt Not Steal."

Had I But Known.

The first thing I did when I went upstairs was hang my nice shirts and skirt and spare jeans in the closet and stash my undies and socks and other clothes in the dresser. I hooked my toiletries bag over the doorknob, piled up my books on the top of the dresser.

I'd thought to bring some sticky-tack, so I was able to hang my posters: Picasso over my bed, Lindsey Lohan in *Mean Girls* on the side wall, and Orlando Bloom in *Pirates of the Caribbean* on the far wall, so I'd see him first thing when I woke up in the morning.

Then I leaned back in my La-Z-Boy and fired up my trusty MacBook to check my email.

When I clicked on the Wi-Fi icon at the top of the screen, though, I got a message telling me there was no network available.

I hadn't thought of that.

No cable, no wireless—what was this place, a prehistoric cave?

And what was I supposed to do without email, without Instant Messenger, without Instagram, without Snapchat?

Curse you, Morty!

Totally disgusted, I went down to the third floor to brush my teeth and rub Clearasil on my T zone, then scooted back upstairs, changed into my jammies, and hopped into bed. I breezed through two medium Sudokus—in ink; pencil is for wimps!—and read a chapter of *Murder in Mesopotamia*, then switched off the bedside lamp and went to sleep.

June's Log: June 3

It was a little before eight when I woke up. Outside my window, rain fell in heavy sheets, and the sky was a leaden gray. Breakfast was at nine on Saturdays and Sundays, Mrs. Smedleigh had told me, so I had an hour before I needed to be downstairs.

I usually do yoga in the mornings, but I'd missed the last couple of days in all the excitement of court and settling into the Roomy Toilet. It was time to get back into my routine.

After changing into a leotard and tying my hair back in a ponytail with my favorite scrunchie, I started out as always with some shoulder stretches, then moved from the Cat and Cow Pose into the Cat Tilt to loosen up my back and spine. A minute of the Mountain Pose got me centered, and after that, I did about twenty minutes of Crow and Cobra and Downward Facing Dog, then finished up with two minutes of Corpse Pose.

When I was done, I put my palms together, fingers pointing to the ceiling and thumbs just touching my lower lip, bowed very slightly, and said a respectful "Namaste."

Then I grabbed a towel and shot down to the third floor for a quick shower, back up to the attic to dry my hair and slip into jeans and a T-shirt, and down again, barely pausing on the second-floor landing to wave to Jeff, who was standing in front of the bathroom mirror, shaving noisily with an electric razor.

Phil, Libby, Moonchild, and Miss Roberts were already busy with breakfast, which was waffles and real maple syrup this morning, with fresh fruit salad on the side.

"Are you feeling okay, June?" Phil asked. "You're all flushed."

"I'm fine," I said. "I just did my yoga, and I guess it really gets my blood circulating."

"You do yoga?" Libby enthused. "That's great! Maybe you can teach me a little sometime? I've always wanted to learn."

"Awesome," I said. "I'm all over that."

"I'm a jogger, myself. I go out every morning, early. You're welcome to join me, if you want."

"I should," I said, passing up the waffles but piling my plate with pieces of cantaloupe and honeydew and pineapple and a little bunch of grapes. "If I got more aerobic exercise, maybe I'd work up more of an appetite. I just don't really like to run, though."

"Yogurt's cool," Moonchild said. "It'd go good with this fruit."

The silence that met this remark was deafening, and I had to stop myself from asking my stoned-out fellow tenant if there was *intelligent* life on his planet, too.

"Um," I said, as Moonchild obliviously went on spooning melon balls between his beard and mustache, "so there's no wireless connection here in the house?"

"Have you kids started calling it a wireless again?" Mrs. Smedleigh asked, coming in through the kitchen archway with a fresh pot of coffee, the dozen gaudy bangle bracelets on her wrists clattering noisily with every step. "I just can't keep up with your vocabulary. Anyway, there's a radio in the kitchen, and television in the parlor."

"I remember wireless," Miss Roberts sighed. "When I was a little girl back in Walla Walla, the whole family used to gather around our beautiful Philco and listen to *The Lux Radio Theater* and *The Smiths of San Fernando*, Milton Berle and Jack Benny and—"

She went on listing programs and performers, some of which I recognized from conversations with Pops, some I'd never heard of. This was the first time I'd seen Miss Roberts smiling, and it was a much better look for her than her usual dour, sour expression.

As she reminisced, Jeff came into the dining room carrying the jacket to his gray-pinstriped suit, hung it over the back of his chair, and sat. "Sorry to interrupt," he said, "but what are we talking about? It sounds wonderful."

"It *was* wonderful," Miss Roberts said dreamily, and then she blinked twice and rejoined the rest of us in the Twenty-First Century. "We are talking about the Golden Age of Radio, Mr. Montague, when—"

"Actually, *I'm* sorry to interrupt," I said, "but what I was asking about was wireless *internet*? So I can check my email on my laptop?"

I immediately wished I'd kept my big mouth shut, because the smile disappeared from Miss Roberts' face, which restored the twenty years her upturned lips had removed from her appearance. She closed back in on herself and turned her attention silently to her breakfast.

Once she understood what it was I was asking about, Mrs. Smedleigh confirmed that there was, in fact, no Wi-Fi in the house, as I'd suspected. There was an unused phone jack in the parlor, though, right next to the TV, and I was welcome to plug into that.

So I'd be doing my web surfing via dial up for the duration of my sentence?

Oh, goody. And, parenthetically, was dial up still even a thing? I had no idea.

Heavy steps came down the stairs, and a moment later, Dr. Le Groth entered the dining room and took his seat at the head of the table. He unfolded a paper napkin and laid it carefully on his lap, poured himself a cup of coffee and took a cautious sip, then set the cup down, folded his hands together, and leaned forward.

He hadn't said a word as yet, but there was a grim expression on his face as he examined each of us in turn, and our conversations died away, leaving the room dead quiet except for Fido, who was lapping milk from his yellow bowl, which Mrs. Smedleigh had set just inside the archway leading back to the kitchen.

Finally, he spoke. "Good morning," he said. "I'm afraid something rather serious has happened. Someone has been inside my room."

Jeff looked up from buttering a waffle. "Excuse me?"

"My room," Dr. Le Groth repeated. "Has one of you gone into my room?"

"Certainly not!" Miss Roberts exclaimed.

"It wasn't me, man!" said Moonchild.

"Are you sure it was one of us?" asked Libby.

"What makes you think someone's been in your room?" said Phil.

The doctor cleared his throat. "My clock radio," he said. "I keep it on the night table beside my bed. I set it every night before I retire."

"Your radio?" said Miss Roberts. "That's an odd coincidence. We were just—"

"Seven o'clock, every morning," Libby confirmed. "I hear it go off sometimes, right over my head."

Dr. Le Groth frowned. "Why haven't you mentioned that it bothers you? I would gladly lower the volume."

"Oh, it doesn't *bother* me, Doctor. I'm usually out doing my run by six at the latest. If I'm back in my room at seven, though, I hear it click on. You listen to that talk station, right?"

"Indeed. But this morning, it failed to wake me—and, when I awoke in my own good time, I turned my head to see if there had perhaps been a power failure while I slept—and, in fact, the radio was gone."

"But you set it last night?" Jeff asked.

"Absolutely. I remember quite distinctly. I turned it on, and then I switched out my light and went to sleep."

"Then," I said slowly, "you're saying that somebody unlocked your door sometime last night, while you were sleeping—"

"I never lock my door," the doctor corrected me. "I don't think any of us do."

"So somebody snuck into your room without making enough noise to wake you up, found his way to your night table in the dark, unplugged your radio—"

"How would you know it needed to be unplugged, young lady?"

"I—" I narrowed my eyes. "It's a clock radio," I said. "They plug into the wall. Don't they?"

"I've never seen one that doesn't," said Libby.

"I don't think I have, either," Jeff said—and Libby gave him a dirty look, as if he'd disagreed with her.

"In any event," Dr. Le Groth said, "yes, someone apparently invaded my bedroom in the night, unplugged my radio, and stole away with it. The radio itself cost me twenty or twenty-five dollars, that's not the point. The point is: I am outraged that one of you would enter my room without permission and—"

"I swear, man, it wasn't me!" Moonchild protested.

"I didn't do it," said Phil.

"Didn't do what, dear?" Mrs. Smedleigh asked, coming through the archway with a plate piled high with more waffles.

"Someone seems to have stolen the doctor's radio from his room," said Miss Roberts stiffly.

"In the middle of the night," Jeff added, "while he was in bed asleep."

Our landlady set the plate down in the center of the table and wiped her hands on her apron. "That's absurd," she said. "How could that be possible? And why would anyone want to run the risk of being caught stealing something as silly as a radio?"

"Nevertheless," Dr. Le Groth said, "my radio was on my bedside table when I went to sleep last night, and this morning it is gone. Ergo, someone must have entered my room while I slept and taken it."

"But who would *do* such a thing?"

"I'm sure I don't know," he said. "I will note, however, that there has never been a theft in this house during the month I have lived here, and—"

"I've been here for two years," Jeff said, "longer than any of you, and nothing's ever been stolen in all that time."

"—and now we have two new tenants," the doctor continued, looking meaningfully from me to Phil Marlowe, "and suddenly my radio has been—"

"Hey, wait a minute!" Phil cried. "Don't look at *me*. I slept like a baby all night and never left my room."

"Same here," I said. "I don't even know which room yours *is*."

"Well, if it wasn't either of *you*, Miss Knight or Mr. Marlowe, then who was it? If you can tell me that, then I will gladly withdraw the accu—the suggestion."

And, without eating a bite of breakfast, he stood up, crumpled his napkin, tossed it angrily onto his untouched plate, and stalked out of the room and up the stairs.

Great.

I'd been emancipated for all of forty-eight hours—*less!*—and here I was suspected of being a thief.

Just perfect.

I thought the situation over in my attic room after breakfast, the rain steadily pelting the Roomy Toilet's peaked roof with a sound like keys clattering on an old typewriter, and finally came to the conclusion that the best way to take out the stain on my character would to figure out what really *had* happened to Dr. Le Groth's radio.

I mean, I was an "ectress," wasn't I, first the Yummy Nibbles spokeskid and now starring as the Emancipated Teenager at a boarding house near you?

Well, if I was *really* going to prove myself, it looked like my next role was going to have to be Nancy Drew.

It was Sunday, so those of Mrs. Smedleigh's tenants who were gainfully employed most likely had the day off, and the rain would probably keep everyone indoors. That meant I'd need to be careful about where I went and what I did, but it seemed to me that I at least ought to be able to figure out the lay of the land.

And so, wishing I had the Hardy Boys along to help, I set out to do some basic reconnaissance…

Standing in the entryway with my back to the front door, the parlor was on my left and the dining room was to the right through a set of off-white French doors. On the far side of the dining room, an archway led back to the downstairs bathroom and kitchen. To begin sleuthing, I wandered back that way—and found Mrs. Smedleigh standing at the sink in her lobster apron, washing the breakfast dishes.

"Hello, dear," she said brightly. "You're all settled in?"

"Yes, ma'am, thanks. It's a beautiful house."

"Why, thank *you*, June, how sweet. Would you like an Oreo?" She nodded down and to her right. "They're in that cabinet, with Fido's food and bowl."

"I'm pretty full from breakfast," I said. "Another time, though?"

"You just help yourself, dear, *any* time."

I looked around the kitchen. It was a large, cozy space, with copper pots and pans hanging from a metal frame that was attached to the ceiling by chains at the four corners, an oversized baby-blue Westinghouse refrigerator beside a matching Hotpoint gas range, and dishes stacked up haphazardly on a baker's rack along the eastern wall, whose large window looked across a narrow side yard and driveway to the house next door. A dish of lavender on the countertop next to the sink made the room smell like a meadow.

There was a sliding glass door leading out to the back yard. It was half-open to let a breeze circulate, so the winged plastic-cling silhouettes on each of the two big panes, meant to warn off the birds, seemed to overlap each other. I assumed that the closed wooden door in the west wall had a pantry behind it, but then I noticed that there weren't any hinges visible, which told me it opened away from me, not toward me.

"Where does that lead?" I asked.

Mrs. S turned her head to follow my gaze. "Ah, that's my room," she said. "It used to be Horace's study—my first Mr. Smedlee, you know?—but when he passed away and I decided to turn our home into a boarding house, I converted it into a little *appartement* for myself. This way, my tenants don't feel like I'm hovering over them every moment."

There were a couple of open spice jars sitting on the counter, and I picked one up and sniffed gingerly at its contents. Cinnamon.

"You know, I didn't take Dr. Le Groth's radio," I said, looking down at the jar instead of at the landlady.

"Oh, goodness, of *course* you didn't, dear! I never for a moment thought you had. That man!" She shook her head and made a *tsk* noise with her tongue. "I don't know him all that well, June—he hasn't even been here a month—but he seems a bit, well, absent-minded to me. It wouldn't surprise me if it turns out he just *moved* his silly radio for some reason and forgot having done so. I expect he'll pop downstairs any moment, full of apologies."

The doctor hadn't seemed absent-minded to *me*—but then I'd only been in the house for a couple of days. Maybe she was right. That'd cut my career as a detective short, but it'd sure take the pressure off.

The second and third floors of the Roomy Toilet were pretty much carbon copies: each had two bedrooms on the north side overlooking the back yard, plus one bedroom, a bathroom, and the stairwell on the south, facing Smedley Street. Mrs. Smedleigh had told me who was in each room when she'd introduced them to me at breakfast on Saturday, but my memory wasn't photographic like Phil's. I did remember that Moonchild was in the front room on the third floor, and I'd seen Libby going in and out of the northwest bedroom on the second floor, and she'd mentioned this morning that Dr. Le Groth was right upstairs from her, which put him in the northwest corner of the third floor. That left Jeff, Phil, and Miss Roberts in the second-floor front and second- and third-floor northeast rooms, and it seemed logical to pinpoint which of them was where. I could have just asked Mrs. Smedleigh, but I didn't think of that until after I'd already left the kitchen, and I didn't want to go back and bother her again.

Since Miss Roberts was retired, there was a chance she'd be in her room, especially since the rain was still coming down pretty steadily. I knocked at random on the second-floor-front room's closed door—and, sure enough, immediately heard footsteps shuffle across the carpet and the spinster's voice say a curt, "Yes?"

"Miss Roberts?"

"Yes?"

"It's June, ma'am. I was wondering if, um, if you wanted to talk about giving me lessons, like you said?"

There was a moment's pause, then: "I am resting, young lady. Perhaps we can discuss the matter this evening."

"Oh, okay, sure. I'm sorry I disturbed you."

She didn't reply. I heard her shuffle away again and then the creak of bedsprings.

Well, at least I could add her name and location to my mental map.

On the third floor, the door to the northeast bedroom was open, and I could see Phil Marlowe sitting at a small wooden desk set against the window that looked out on the back yard—which put Jeff in the last remaining room, in the northeast corner of the second floor.

Phil had his back to me, and he was bent over a little notebook, busily scribbling.

I didn't want to bug him, but either some sixth sense told him I was standing out in the hall or a floorboard creaked beneath the carpet, and he straightened up and turned around and saw me.

"June!" he said, and he didn't seem upset to be interrupted. He folded his notebook shut and slipped it into a drawer of the desk. "Come in!"

The room was kind of a mess: cardboard boxes on the floor, a big suitcase open on the unmade bed, nothing on the walls except a framed old picture of fishing boats in a small-town harbor that looked like it'd been painted by the same starving artist who'd done the village scene I'd taken down from the wall of my attic room and hidden away in the closet.

"Sit down," Phil said, then realized that he was already occupying the room's only chair. He got to his feet and ushered me into it with a stagey two-handed wave, zipped his suitcase shut, and moved it to the floor so he could perch on the edge of the bed.

"There's no place like home," he said and laughed with delight when I clicked my heels three times in response. "I didn't realize kids your age still watch the classics."

"Oh, I love 'em," I said eagerly. "My father owns an antiques store, and he's got all kinds of old movie posters and stuff. We've got like a million silent comedies and Cary Grants and Hitchcocks in our Netflix queue, and we—"

I stopped myself, suddenly remembering why I was living in the Roomy Toilet in the first place.

Phil nodded as if he understood. "Mrs. Smedleigh told me about the emancipation," he said. So, he *did* understand. "You don't sound like a girl who's having major trouble with her parents."

He seemed like such a nice guy. I wanted to trust him with the truth, but Morty had made it abundantly clear I was to keep our publicity stunt a secret from *everyone*, even my friends.

"I—I don't really want to talk about it."

"Change of subject," he said immediately. "Um, how do you like being a suspect in our burglary?"

"Do you really think Dr. Le Groth's radio was *stolen*?" I said gratefully. "Maybe he just—I don't know—he's kind of old. Maybe he just misplaced it or something."

"I don't how you 'misplace' a clock radio," Phil said. "No, somebody probably swiped it, and I suppose it must have been one of us. *You* didn't take it, did you?"

"No way! Did you?"

He shook his head. "I don't even listen to the radio in my *car*," he said. "I've got Apple CarPlay and an iPhone, and that does me just fine."

"I have an iPhone, too, with like ten million gigs of memory, and I don't even have it *halfway* full. What do I need a radio for?"

"Exactly. Anyway, apparently nobody ever locks their doors here, so *anyone* could have slipped into his room and taken it."

"If he's telling the truth, though," I said, "he was *in* the room sleeping when it was stolen."

"Can you see Miss Roberts tiptoeing into the doctor's bedroom in the middle of the night?"

I giggled. "I'll bet Moonchild could have done it."

"If he didn't fall over his own feet and wake up the whole house."

"Or Jeff. He seems pretty smooth."

"Or Libby—don't be a sexist."

He was talking to me like an adult, not a child, and I found myself really *liking* him.

I only had *his* word that he wasn't himself the radio swiper, though, and he *was* the newest tenant in the house.

If I was going to catch the thief and clear myself from suspicion, I knew I couldn't trust that *anyone* was telling me the truth.

* * *

After an Italian dinner starring an odd pasta Mrs. Smedleigh called *bigoli*—sort of a hollow spaghetti, like drinking straws made out of noodles—a big salad and plenty of garlic bread, another matching armchair had magically appeared in the parlor, turning the grouping of two chairs by the western wall into a trio. Phil settled into one of those and scribbled notes in his little memo pad until Libby came in and parked herself beside him. Pretty soon, the two of them were deep in conversation.

I, meanwhile, was standing in front of the wall of bookshelves, ostensibly checking out the offerings on display—most of which were by authors I'd never heard of and looked about as interesting as a collection of math books—but really using that as an opportunity to check out my fellow tenants while they didn't know I was watching them. I'd take down a random volume, lean against the shelves, and page through it idly, looking up as if in thought to observe the rest of them.

Encyclopedia Brown probably would have cracked the case in thirty seconds. I, however, was clearly not that good.

Libby and Phil seemed completely engrossed in their conversation, two attractive twenty-somethings thrown together by the accident of living under the same boarding-house roof. Neither one of them looked like a master criminal relaxing after a hard day of burglary.

Jeff, on the other hand, was alone on the sofa, flipping so quickly through a magazine it was obvious he wasn't paying any attention whatsoever to the pages he was turning. He seemed mad at the world—but was this the behavior of someone suffering from guilt pangs...or heartburn? I had no idea. Finally, he quit pretending to read, threw the magazine back onto the coffee table, and stormed up to his room.

Moonchild was missing in action, but Miss Roberts and Dr. Le Groth were in their usual places. She was back at her cross-stitching, and he was grumbling about his missing radio. I remembered catching a look last night at the words spelled out on Miss Roberts' canvas: "Thou Shalt Not Steal."

How ironic.

Or *was* it irony? I already knew that Libby could hear the doctor's radio from her room, directly beneath him. Miss Roberts was across the hall from Libby. Was it possible *she* had heard it, too, and it had annoyed her to the point where she'd found herself thinking about swiping it? Had she started the sampler to try to talk herself out of the theft? Had she finally lost control of herself, snuck upstairs while the house was asleep, slipped through the doctor's unlocked door, and—

Miss Roberts? Sneaking into people's rooms and stealing?

I looked up from the book I wasn't reading to find her gazing directly at me, as if she'd heard me thinking about her.

"Young lady," she said sternly.

"Yes, ma'am?"

"Come here, child."

I closed the book and slipped it back into place, then stepped over and stood obediently beside her chair.

She looked up at me expectantly.

The silence lengthened.

"Ma'am?" I said at last.

"I am waiting," she said.

I cocked my head quizzically. "Ma'am?"

She sighed. "This afternoon," she said, slowly and carefully, as if she was talking to a new immigrant who didn't understand English, "you asked to speak with me regarding lessons."

"Oh, *that*, right. Um, the thing is, I was thinking about it afterwards, and I decided that, see, it's Sunday, and summer break starts on Tuesday, anyway. So I figured I might as well just take the summer off. And then, if I'm still emancipated in September, I think I'll just go back to regular school."

She pondered that. "Are you thinking that you might *not* be?"

I hope not, I thought, but what I said was, "Well, you never know, you know? But thanks for offering, Miss Roberts, really."

As I made my escape, I happened to glance down and noticed that she'd finished last night's sampler and was already hard at work on a new one. Again there were two gray tablets in the center of the hoop, but this time they bore the numeral 9 and the text: "Thou Shalt Not Covet Thy Neighbor's Goods."

How appropriate could you get? She was apparently working her way through the Ten Commandments in numerical order, and, given what had happened at the Roomy Toilet, her cross-stitching commented on current events like the intertitles in a silent movie.

I found myself wondering if any of the neighbors had wives. If so, tomorrow was shaping up to be the most interesting day yet of my emancipation.

Thinking about current events reminded me that I hadn't checked my email, so I trooped up to the attic for my MacBook, power adapter, and retractable modem cable. Back in the parlor, I borrowed a cushion from the sofa and set it against the east wall next to the TV, plugged everything into the appropriate ports and outlets, and managed, after a little experimenting, to get myself online.

The usual junk had weaseled its way through my spam filter, but there was also some personal stuff in my inbox: chatty messages from my best friends Allie and Brenna, a couple of e-newsletters I subscribe to, and a note from Pops telling me he got some "new ones" in at the shop and inviting me to come by the next day and pick out the ones I wanted. I wrote back to Pops to tell him I would and was about to reply to Allie when there she was:

ALLIEKAT6201: junie! ☺

YummyJune: hihi!

ALLIEKAT6201: did you really move out?

YummyJune: yupyup

ALLIEKAT6201: what happened? ru ok?

YummyJune: i'm fine. long story

ALLIEKAT6201: where ru?

YummyJune: it's like a rooming house. pretty cool

ALLIEKAT6201: ru eating ok?

YummyJune: yeah, great food!

ALLIEKAT6201: no BRAT diet for junie?

YummyJune: absolutely! beetles, roaches, ants, and termites!

ALLIEKAT6201: eeuw, gross!

YummyJune: when can we get together? so much to tell you!

ALLIEKAT6201: last day of school is tues. half moon on weds?

YummyJune: sounds good!

ALLIEKAT6201: i'll tell brennie. hey, sorry, g2g! ☹

YummyJune: k, cya!

After filling up on celebrity gossip at my usual websites, I decided to put on my Sherlock Holmes hat and Google the Roomy Toilet's tenants. Maybe I could ferret out some information that'd help me deduce the identity of the thief….

I started by typing "Phillip Marlowe" in the little search window and got a message reading: "Did you mean *Philip* Marlowe?" When I clicked on that spelling, the search engine took 0.04 seconds to offer me two hundred and eighty-one thousand hits. Eek. I surfed through the first several pages of possibilities, and they all seemed to be in agreement that Philip Marlowe was—go figure!—a character in a series of private-eye novels by Raymond Chandler. Well, wait a minute. Was it possible that Mrs. Smedleigh—or Dr. Le Groth?—had hired a PI to investigate the theft of the doctor's radio? Was our Phil really just an ordinary Tom or Dick or Harry, using a famous fictional detective's name as a cover?

No, that didn't make sense: Phil moved in last night, before the theft was even discovered.

Next, I tried "Liberty N Justice," and was steered to the website of a Christian rock band by that name. (Well, with an apostrophe after the N, but close enough.) They had a song called "Another Nail" available for download, and I listened to it over my headphones and kind of liked it. A little more heavily metal than my usual taste, but interesting, and I skipped over to Apple Music and bookmarked their *Welcome to the Revolution* album for later listening.

Searching on "Libby Justice" produced a "Libby Justice Court" in Libby, Montana, and, oddly enough, a Libby Justice in Wellington, New Zealand, who had apparently represented some of the actors playing Hobbits in the *Lord of the Ring* movies, plus a bunch of editorials arguing that some politician named Scooter Libby either did or didn't get justice in his 2005 court case, but none of that seemed especially germane.

"Jeffrey Montague" brought up two hundred and sixteen hits, and they were a pretty mixed bag. The good news was that three articles in our town newspaper, the *Straight Shooter*, quoted "local attorney Jeffrey Montague" on legal cases he was working on. None of them had anything to do with radio, though, nor did they mention Dr. Le Groth or any of Mrs. Smedleigh's other boarders. I also found a Director of Undergraduate Programs in the School of Tourism and Hospitality Management at Temple University with the same name, an employee of the Mental Health & Addiction Services unit of the SE Connecticut Mental Health Authority, and a member of the Adjunct Theater Faculty at Washburn University in Topeka, Kansas. There were several mentions of a swimmer in the 1999 AAU Junior Olympics, and I even found a reference to Jeffrey Montague as the 1995 Slytherin House Captain in a piece of Harry Potter fan fiction by someone named "Firesword."

Which led me to try "Moonchild" next. And, as Morty would have said, "Oy vey." I got, like, four hundred and fifty thousand hits—it would have taken me a hundred years to check them all out. What was his real name again? Andrew Something? I couldn't remember. I typed "Andrew Moonchild" into the search window, and that narrowed the field to thirty thousand items, starting with a photograph of some lady reclining on what looked like a giant stone carving of a crescent moon, titled "Moon Child" and copyrighted by Andrew Looney. *Our* Moonchild was definitely loony, but the connection seemed awfully thin.

At nine o'clock, Dr. Le Groth set down his book and asked if I minded him turning on the TV to watch the news. "I would normally go up and listen to it in my room," he said, "but, ahem, that's not an option this evening."

"No, go ahead," I said. "I don't mind."

"The sound won't disturb you?"

"Nuh-uh, I'm fine."

He switched on the set, turned the volume politely low, and returned to his armchair. I couldn't see the screen from where I was sitting, but the anchorman's affected voice just *sounded* blow-dried as he started talking about some peace conference being held somewhere to try to end the violence that was happening somewhere else.

When I typed in "Simeon Le Groth," I got this message: "Your search did not match any documents." That was odd. I tried "Simon Le Groth" and "S. Le Groth," and Simeon and Simon and S. "LeGroth," without the space. No hits, no hits, no hits, no hits, no hits. Interesting. I even went to the websites for several local hospitals, but no Simeon or S. Le Groth was listed in any of their staff directories.

And Miss Roberts? I realized that I had no idea what her first name was, and I didn't even bother Googling "Miss Roberts." Talk about a waste of time!

"Locally," the news anchor said, "a spokeswoman for the city police department announced that there are no leads in the daring daylight robbery of a second area bank, which followed closely on the heels of Friday's—"

The rest of the sentence was drowned out by a roar from the dining room. I leaned over to look through the French doors and saw Mrs. Smedleigh wielding an upright vacuum that looked like it dated all the way back to the Hoover Administration.

"Can you not do that some other time, madam?" Dr. Le Groth shouted. "I am *trying* to watch the news!" It was the first time I'd heard him raise his voice above a low rumble, and Mrs. S immediately switched off the offending machine and bustled into the parlor.

"I'm sorry, doctor," she said. "I didn't realize you had the television on. Why aren't you—oh, of course." She shook her head sadly and, wiping her hands on her apron, went back out again.

A different voice was predicting more rain through tomorrow morning, then sunny skies and higher temperatures for the rest of the week.

I typed "Prunella Smedleigh," "Prunella Smedlee," and "Prunella Smeddlea" into the search box and came up with nothing, nothing, and more nothing, respectively. I even tried "Prunella Smedley," just for the heck of it, but there was nothing there, either.

As I was about to give up and put my laptop away, another chat window popped onto my screen.

bReNaNdStImPy: hey, gf! what's the haps?

That was Brenna, my second-best friend.

Okay, I know this is going to sound horrible, but I don't really *like* Brenna all that much. When we were kids, she and Allie and I were inseparable. Even when Mom and Pops put me into homeschooling, the three of us continued to hang out together as often as we could, and Brenna's fine in a group. One-on-one, though, it's like she regresses back to about eleven years old, and her immaturity kind of gives me a pain. I mean, look at her screen name! Ren and Stimpy were funny for about fifteen minutes back when my parents were kids, but they've been *over* since Y2K at least.

YummyJune: sorry, bren, i'm in the middle of something. we'll get together and catch up soon, k?

bReNaNdStImPy: sure thing, sweetie! :-p

bReNaNdStImPy: :::blowing kisses:::

YummyJune: nighty night! ;-*

I clicked the chat window shut.

"What's the haps?" and "sweetie" and blown kisses?

For Christmas, I was definitely going to have to see if I could find a clue in that girl's size.

Once again about to close up shop, I changed my mind and, for the first time ever, Googled "June Knight."

And guess what?

It turns out there was a June Knight who was born in 1913, introduced Cole Porter's classic song "Begin the Beguine" in *Jubilee*, a 1934 Broadway musical, played leads through the Thirties in a dozen Hollywood movies I'd never heard of, and was billed seventh (behind Jack Benny, Eleanor Powell, Robert Taylor, Una Merkel, Sid Silvers and Buddy Ebsen) in *Broadway Melody of 1936*, which was nominated for the Best Picture Oscar. And, get this, she passed away on June 16, 1987, exactly twenty-three years *to the day* before I was born! Weird!

Google Images provided some pictures of her. A color close-up on the cover of a 1937 issue of *Picturegoer* magazine showed her with a gorgeous smile and these amazingly thin eyebrows—she was credited as the author of the issue's cover story, "Some TRUTHS about ROBERT TAYLOR"—and an undated black-and-white pinup shot had her in permed blond hair and a *really* tight white dress with a hemline so high you could practically see her underwear.

So, although I hadn't found out anything useful about any of my fellow boarders, at least I'd learned there was some precedent for a girl named June Knight making it big in show biz. I didn't have any trouble being happy with that!

I opened my eyes in darkness and reached for my watch on the nightstand. Fumbling, I found the little button on the side and pressed it, and the Indiglo readout told me it was almost one in the morning.

Somewhere, the central A/C clicked on, and there was a soft whoosh of chilled air circulating through the vents. Otherwise, the house was completely silent.

I had to pee.

As quietly as possible, so as not to wake anyone up, I crept down the stairs from the attic to the third floor. The landing was dimly lit by a single nightlight plugged into an outlet in the narrow strip of wall that separated Dr. Le Groth's room from Phil Marlowe's, just enough illumination to show me that the bathroom door was open, the bathroom dark and unoccupied.

Inside, I pulled the door shut and groped for the light switch.

Before my fingers found it, I thought I heard a noise out in the hallway. I eased the door back open a fraction of an inch and put an eye to the crack.

Across the hall, Moonchild was just leaving his room. He was wearing cutoff jeans and a T-shirt. Even in the dim light of the hallway, the letters on his shirt were big enough I could read their message: "MAKE LOVE, NOT WAR." He looked both ways, saw the coast was clear, and crept down the stairs, his leather moccasins completely soundless on the wooden floor.

My heart pounding in my chest, I slipped out of my slippers and followed him, stepping as lightly as I could to make sure the floorboards didn't creak. I expected him to continue on down to the ground floor—he probably just had the munchies, I figured, and was heading for the kitchen to fix himself a midnight snack—but he surprised me. He stopped on the second-floor landing and tiptoed in slow motion over to Miss Roberts' room. I could see a light under the bottom of her door—she was awake. Maybe I was imagining it, but I thought I could just hear the sound of crying.

Moonchild brushed his long, straggly hair back from his right ear and leaned against the door, listening intently.

What was he up to?

I stood in the stairwell for five minutes, watching him. I don't think I'd ever seen him stand still for that long at a stretch. Finally, I realized that *I* was having trouble standing still. I *really* had to pee, so I gave up my stakeout and crept back upstairs.

Just as I reached the bathroom, I heard a doorknob turn. I slipped inside and again peeked through the narrow aperture between door and jamb.

Phil Marlowe's door swung slowly open, and Phil tiptoed out, barefoot, in a pair of plaid pjs. He snuck silently next door to Dr. Le Groth's room and tapped very quietly. The door inched open, and Phil melted inside and carefully closed it behind him.

A chill marched up my spine, and I don't think it was just the air-conditioning.

What was going *on* at the Roomy Toilet?

June's Log: June 4

"What do you know about Dr. Le Groth?" I asked Mrs. Smedleigh, when she came out of the kitchen with a tray of thermoses and pitchers and jugs. She had on a satiny purple jogging suit this morning, with shiny gold stripes and big plastic jewels sewn across the front of the jacket. A few minutes earlier, when I'd clattered down the stairs from my room and first seen her in that get-up, I'd asked her if, like Libby, she liked to run. "Only errands, dear," she'd said with a smile.

Now, as she set her tray down on the dining room table and began to put things in their proper places, she said, "He's attending some kind of seminar today."

"No, I mean, what do you *know* about him? I tried looking him up on my computer, but I couldn't find anything at all. He's not listed at any of the hospitals in town."

She absently tucked a loose strand of hair behind her ear. "Well, perhaps he's in private practice?"

"He doesn't show up on the internet at *all*," I said. "That's *awfully* private."

"Well, I'm sure there's an explanation, dear. Why don't you ask him at supper?"

"Maybe I will," I said.

I heard footsteps on the stairs, and a moment later, Libby and Jeff came in together.

"I will have it on your desk by noon," she said tightly, circling around the dining table and settling in beside me.

"But the meeting is at *eleven*," he said, taking his place across from her.

It was Monday morning, and they were dressed for the office, Libby in a pretty coral-skirted suit over a scoop-necked white blouse and Jeff in a sharp gray pinstripe, pale-blue shirt, and power tie.

"Is there any way—?" Jeff began, but Libby completely blew him off, turning to me and chirping, "Good morning, June! And what are you up to today?"

"If it ever stops raining," I said, "I'm going into town to visit my—"

I was about to say "father," but then I realized that maybe I shouldn't. After all, the whole point of my living at the Roomy Toilet was that I was supposed to be *distancing* myself from my parents.

"—my friends," I finished.

"That sounds like fun," she said.

And then Phil and Moonchild and Miss Roberts all came in and took their seats, and Mrs. Smedleigh came out of the kitchen with a giant bowl of something I had no idea what it was and, since Dr. Le Groth wasn't there, started her trip around the table with me.

"That looks, um, great," I said, examining the lumpy off-white stuff in my bowl suspiciously. "What, uh, what is it?"

"It's *flocons d'avoine*, dear," she said cheerfully, moving on to Libby. "That's French."

"It's oatmeal, man," Moonchild whispered across the table, his hand cupped over his mouth. "Put some sugar on it."

"Thanks," I whispered back, and followed his advice.

"When's your next commercial coming out, June?" asked Phil, who was dressed for a hard day of commodity selling in a light-brown linen sports jacket over a yellow T-shirt and khakis.

"I don't know," I said. "It ought to be soon, I think—it's been a couple of months since I did the last one."

"America needs to be reminded at regular intervals to stock up on Tasty Nibbles," Jeff said sullenly, pouring coffee.

"Yummy," I said.

"I'm glad you like it, dear," said Mrs. Smedleigh, spooning oatmeal into Phil's bowl.

Under the table, Libby kicked my leg, then nodded meaningfully at my untouched breakfast. I quickly dipped my spoon and took a bite. "Mmm," I said, surprised. "This is pretty yummy, too! I meant the dog food, though. It's *Yummy* Nibbles."

"Oh, yes, I bought those once by mistake and tried giving them to Fido." She shook her head at the memory. "Which reminds me, this is a funny coincidence: Fido's bowl seems to be missing."

"You gave dog food to a *cat*, man?" said Moonchild. "That's, like, *weird*."

"Did he like them?" Libby asked.

"He did not. I'm sure they're very popular with dogs, June, but Fido turned up his nose at them. I dumped them out and gave him some canned tuna instead, but he wouldn't even eat *that* until I'd washed the smell of the Nimmy—"

"Yummy," I said. "Yummy Nibbles. I don't know why everybody always gets that wrong."

"—the Yummy Nibbles out of his bowl."

At that moment, the telephone rang, and she dashed back to the kitchen to answer it.

"Are you sure the missing bowl's just a coincidence?" Jeff wondered, waggling his eyebrows like Groucho Marx and tapping ash off an imaginary cigar. "Maybe our Mystery Burglar has struck again?"

"Don't be an idiot, Mr. Montague," Libby scoffed. "Who on earth would want to steal a food dish from a cat?"

Phil leaned over and whispered something in Libby's ear, and her hand flew up to her mouth just a second too late to hide a smile.

"I don't like secrets," Miss Roberts announced. "They're very rude." She stood up abruptly and left the table, her oatmeal barely touched.

As soon as I heard her footsteps on the stairs, I leaned over to Libby and whispered, "Do you know her first name?"

"Miss Roberts?" Libby looked puzzled. "Why, no, I don't." She turned to her left. "Phil, you don't know Miss Roberts' first name, do you?"

"No idea."

"I don't think I ever heard it," mused Jeff. He turned towards the kitchen archway and called, "Mrs. Smedleigh?"

"Coming!" she trilled in reply, and a moment later returned to the dining room. "Telemarketers," she said. "At this hour! Can I offer anyone another helping of *flocons*?"

"It's absolutely the bomb," Jeff told her, "but I couldn't eat another bite. We're trying to remember La Roberts' first name, but none of us seems to know it."

"It's—" She hesitated. "I think it's—" She tapped her upper lip thoughtfully. "Well, isn't that funny?" she said. "I don't think *I* know her Christian name, either."

"It's gotta be on her lease, man, right?" suggested Moonchild.

"Of course!" Mrs. Smedleigh brightened. "What a good idea, Moonchild!" And she scurried off towards the rolltop desk in the parlor.

"You've got unexplored depths, there, podner," Jeff said admiringly.

Moonchild wiped the inside of his bowl with his index finger and sucked up the last molecules of oatmeal. "Hey, I'm not *stupid*, man."

Mrs. Smedleigh was back in a minute, waving a sheet of paper at us. "Here we are," she said and smoothed the page out on the dining room table. She pushed her cat-eye glasses an inch higher up the bridge of her nose and leaned in to scrutinize the lease.

"Well, I never!" she exclaimed. "June, can *you* read this?"

She passed the document across the table, and I took it and squinted closely at the handprinted name at the top of the page and the signature at the bottom.

In both places, the "Roberts" was clear, but the first name preceding it was completely illegible.

The lie I'd come up with at breakfast to cover my planned visit to Pops' antique store reminded me that I hadn't seen Brenna or Allie in almost a week, and that Allie and I had agreed via last night's brief chat session to meet at the Half Moon, our favorite coffee house, on Wednesday afternoon to catch up, and she'd promised to fill Brenna in on the plan. We hadn't set a time, though, so I fetched my laptop from my room, plugged it in, and sent each of them an email suggesting two that afternoon.

There wasn't much in my inbox, and I guess it's true what they say about Monday being a slow news day: even *Teen Vogue* hadn't come up with anything interesting since last night, and I could usually count on them to fill me in on the latest Hollywood scandals and fashion *faux pas*. (That's French!)

I battled an Ultra Hard level of Candy Crush Soda Saga ten times without coming close to beating it—partly, I'm sure, because my heart wasn't really in it. While my hands were mechanically popping bottles and launching flying fish, my brain was busy wrestling with the problem of Dr. Le Groth's missing radio.

I tried to think of it logically, like a Sudoku, where every number *has* to fit neatly into one and only one square. The radio had disappeared from the doctor's square, so it had to have been moved to some *other* square. But which?

If there were any clues to be found, I decided, they would probably be found in the thief's square. I didn't imagine for a moment that the radio would be sitting in plain sight—or Fido's bowl, for that matter—but I was determined to figure out who the guilty party was, and checking the suspects' living quarters was about all the CSI I could think to do.

Libby, Jeff, and Phil had all gone off to work and Dr. Le Groth was at some kind of seminar, but unemployed Moonchild and retired Miss Roberts were probably in their rooms.

Moonchild and Miss Roberts.

Why, I wondered, had Moonchild been listening at Miss Roberts' door last night? And had the stern, no-nonsense spinster actually been *crying*? If her light had been out and her room had been silent, would he have snuck inside and stolen one of *her* possessions? Was Moonchild the Roomy Toilet's Napoleon of Crime?

I shut down my computer and took it back to the attic, and then, full of determination, marched down to the third floor and knocked firmly on the aging hippie's door.

"Just a second," he yelled. There was a series of unidentifiable noises, and then the door swung open a crack.

"Hey, man!" he said when he saw me, and beneath his unkempt beard and mustache his mouth creased into a smile. He had perfect teeth, I noticed, and I was surprised that that surprised me. "What's goin' on?"

"I'm just—I'm worried about Dr. Le Groth's radio," I told him.

"Yeah, that's really weird. And now the cat's bowl is missing, too. C'mon in, man, we'll talk."

He swung the door wide and ushered me in. I'm not sure what I expected Moonchild's room to look like—DayGlo posters and black light and clouds of strawberry incense, I guess—but what I saw was just an ordinary room, pretty much like my own, except he had taupe carpeting where my floor was bare.

"Lemme clear this off," he said, sweeping a pile of papers off the room's only chair and tossing them onto the dresser. "Sit down, man."

He folded himself into a sloppy lotus position on the floor, his back against the bed.

"So it's pretty crazy, stuff getting ripped off, huh?"

"It's scary," I said. "I mean, we're all living together. Aren't we supposed to be *friends*?"

"Brothers and sisters, man, that's the idea, like a little commune, you know? And you don't rip off your family. That's totally whack."

"Do you think this is it, or will there be more thefts?"

He pulled back. "More? Whoa, I didn't even *think* of that. I hope not." He shrugged. "Not much they could find in here."

I looked around the room. He was right: there wasn't much there to steal. The only personal touch was a framed 8 x 10 black-and-white photograph on the night table beside the bed. In the driveway of a small ranch house, a pretty woman in her thirties stood next to a fresh-faced boy about Dylan's age, holding his hand. They were wearing matching jeans and WWJC sweatshirts with some kind of old-time soldier embroidered on the front.

What Would Jesus Conquer?

"Is that you and your mother?"

He reached around and took the picture and held it in his lap, gazing down at it as if it was a window into the distant past—which, I guess, it was.

"Yeah," he said slowly. "Me and mom. Long time ago, man."

"Is she—?"

He sniffed and coughed and put the photo back on his night table and just sat there gazing at it, his head turned away from me, his long stringy hair hiding his face from view.

There was more I wanted to ask him, but he was off in another world. I waited a while, to see if he might come back, and then I got up and went away and pulled the door shut behind me.

Downstairs, I knocked on Miss Roberts' door, but there was no response.

According to Dr. Le Groth, nobody locked their doors at the Roomy Toilet. I considered barging in and searching her room—for the doctor's radio, for Fido's bowl, for an explanation of why she'd been crying last night. What if she was in there, though, and just not answering my knock? Or, even worse, what if she came back while I was in her room?

No, the possibility of getting caught wasn't really the point. The point was that there's a fine line between "investigating" and "snooping," and I wasn't ready to cross it.

Not yet.

The rain fell steadily all morning, and I finished *Murder in Mesopotamia* and started *The Voyage of the Dawn Treader*, which begins with my all-time favorite opening line of any book I've ever read: "There was a boy called Eustace Clarence Scrubb, and he almost deserved it." Now, doesn't *that* tell you everything you need to know about the kid in a dozen words!

By one that afternoon, the rain had finally cleared, and a gorgeous summer sun turned the gray sky a bright blue dotted with Simpsons clouds. I changed into shorts and a halter top and the ladybug earrings my father calls my "Junebugs," left the Roomy Toilet and let my iPhone provide a soundtrack for my stroll into town to visit my iPop at Aunt Teak & Uncle Junque's, the shop he's owned for as long as I can remember.

I'm not really that into antiques. To me, they're all just a bunch of stuff nobody wants. But Pops seems to know what he's doing: he combs the garage sales around town, picks up things I wouldn't have paid a quarter for, then slaps a five-hundred-dollar price tag on them—and sells them. Okay, fine, that's the exception, not the rule, but the shop brings in enough of an income to support the three of us in a style not *quite* the one we all wish we were accustomed to, but close.

The bell over the door jangled as I stepped inside.

"It's me, Pops!" I yelled, and from way back in the storage room, I heard a muffled shout: "I'll be right out, Junie!"

I picked my way past the curved-glass cabinets and vitrines filled with Royal Doulton and Wedgewood and Limoges and flow blue china, cut-glass perfume bottles and bisque figurines and sterling-silver tea services and flatware and compotes, through the familiar jumble of French marquetry writing desks and Victorian marble-top tables, the Eastlake secretaries and Regency *escritoires* and Duncan Phyfe breakfronts and the mahogany Chippendale dining-room set with one of its eight chairs missing, past the caramel-slag panel lamps and Bohemian ruby-cut decanters and the display case filled with fine jewelry and ivory cigarette holders and gold and silver half-hunters and pocket watches. Over my head, the walls were lined with a gallery of framed posters for old movies: Douglas Fairbanks in *The Thief of Baghdad*, Mary Pickford in *Rebecca of Sunnybrook Farm*, Rudolph Valentino in *Son of the Sheik*, Charlie Chaplin in *The Great Dictator*, Buster Keaton in *Sherlock Junior*, Harold Lloyd in *Safety Last*, the Marx Brothers in *Duck Soup*—one of my favorite childhood memories is sitting sandwiched between Mom and Pops on our living-room couch, watching the classics on DVD, my buttery fingers brushing theirs as we scooped popcorn from the bowl on my lap.

As always, Pops' office—a crowded cubicle set between the back of the store and the storage room—was a disaster area. The shop itself is pretty well organized, but the office looks like Auntie Em and Uncle Henry's farm after the tornado.

There was a copy of the *Straight Shooter* on Pops' massive walnut mid-Victorian partners' desk, and I flopped into the tufted black leather spring-back swivel chair and scooped it up eagerly to look for my name. The front page was all about some complicated political scandal in Washington and "Mayor Announces School Cutbacks" and "Bank Robber Strikes Again." I searched all sixteen pages, and there were stories about traffic accidents and summer recreation leagues and movie reviews and comic strips and sports scores and classified ads, but not one single word about "Local Teen Actress Sues Parents, Wins."

I wished Morty's stupid publicity stunt would hurry up and generate some actual publicity already, so I could return home—where I belonged.

It hadn't happened yet, though, and I was starting to wonder if it ever *would*.

I threw down the paper in disgust.

"Something's wrong," said a familiar voice, and I looked up to find my father standing in the doorway, a cardboard box in his hands. Where my mom looks younger than her thirty-eight years, Pops is forty-two, and the Guess-Your-Age-and-Weight guy at the carnival would probably put him a couple years older. The top of his head is pretty much a cue ball, and the fringe of hair around the sides and back is thinning and prematurely gray. His bushy eyebrows and devilish goatee remind you, though, that once upon a time, the man had a head of dark-brown hair, and the chocolate eyes magnified behind the lenses of his black plastic glasses sometimes seem to have X-ray vision, the way they can pierce through all my teenage drama and see straight into my heart.

"Popster!" I said. "No, it's—"

I hesitated. I knew how worried he was about this whole situation, and I didn't want to make things worse. I wanted to spill how I was feeling, though—I just couldn't figure a way into the subject.

He set the box down on top of his desk, put his warm hands on my shoulders, and looked me straight in the eye. "Tell me, Junie Moon."

"Oh, it's just—do you remember that time I came home from school and asked you if I could have permission, just that once, to curse?"

He smiled. "First grade. You were six. Something happened—one of your friends did something?"

"Dan Pappas. I wanted him to come over and play, but he went to

Rachel Shanks' instead."

"And you were so mad, you came bursting into the house and asked your mom and me if you could 'say a swear.'"

"And you guys were so cool: you said I could, but I'd have to eat my words. And Mom made a sheet of Jell-O Jigglers, and we had these alphabet cookie cutters, and I got to cut out a swear and say it out loud and eat the letters."

"Do you remember the word you spelled?"

I had to think a moment, but then it came back to me: "Poop!"

"Yes, indeedy, that was it."

"So then I had to eat poop," I giggled.

"And the next day, you told your friends at school, and half of them went home and told their parents that Junie's mom and dad made her eat poop. We must have gotten a dozen phone calls that evening." He shook his head and chuckled. "What makes you think about that now?"

I folded my arms, sucked in a breath, and blew it out. "Oh, it's just this whole emancipation thing. It makes me want to say a swear."

"Go ahead. Say *two*. This time, I won't even make you eat your words."

I laughed. "No, it's okay. I just hope this doesn't go on much longer." I nodded at the box on his desk. "Is that them?"

He released my shoulders and waved a hand. "Help yourself."

Pops gave me a stereopticon for my last birthday—it's kind of like a View-Master, only old—and he always gives me first crack at the slides when he gets a new batch of them in.

I did some Googling when I got the gift and learned that the Brits and Germans were already experimenting with three-dimensional viewing within about ten or twelve years of the development of wet-plate photography in the early 1820s, but that the basic principle of the device went all the way back to ancient Greece when the mathematician Euclid figured out and proved that the left and right eyes see slightly different versions of the same thing—what we now call binocular, or "two-eyed" vision—and that it's the brain's combining of these two images that allows us to see the world in 3-D.

Anyway, Queen Victoria got totally hooked on what was then called the "stereoscope" at the Crystal Palace Exposition in 1851, and Oliver Wendell Holmes and some other guy came out with an American version during the Civil War, and by the end of the Nineteenth Century, you'd find some sort of stereo viewing device in just about every well-off household on the planet. They weren't just a toy for the kiddies, either—they were sort of like what TV is to us today, allowing people to see the wide world and its curiosities without ever leaving the comfort of their front rooms.

Maybe, given what I do for a living, that's why I got so interested.

The ritzier stereopticons were made of expensive materials and were usually mounted on a stand, but mine is a more middle-class handheld model. There's, like, a headpiece with two square lenses set into it and angled very slightly towards each other and a long flat piece with a crossbar that holds the slides. On each slide—they're maybe seven inches wide and three, three-and-a-half inches tall—there are two photos taken by a special camera that has side-by-side lenses set a couple of inches apart, about the same distance that separates a human's eyes. So you fit a slide onto the crossbar, hold the handle in one hand, and look through the lenses, and your left eye sees only the left-hand photo, and your right eye sees only the right-hand photo. You slide the crossbar away from your face, and the two photos blend into one blurry image. Slide the crossbar slowly closer, and the image comes into focus—and your brain does its thing, and you see the Pyramids of Egypt or the building of the Panama Canal or the devastation left behind by the Great San Francisco Earthquake and Fire of 1906, or whatever, in perfect three dimensions.

There were maybe fifty of the thick rectangular cardboard slides in this new assortment, and I went through them slowly and carefully. A third of them were either totally faded out and worthless or else showed scenes that wouldn't have been any more fun to look at in 3-D than in two dimensions. The rest were really promising, though, and I picked out three to take with me: a 1901 black-and-white shot of Rome, as seen from the dome of St. Peter's Cathedral; a 1902 b/w view of the East Room of the White House, magnificently decorated (according to the printed text on the back) for a state dinner for Germany's Prince Hendrick; and a hand-tinted but undated shot of a long row of what I think must have been cypresses stretching into the distance, with the cemetery of Palermo's Convent of the Cappuccini off to the right side of the frame.

"These are great, Pops," I said. "Where did you get them?"

"The usual," he said. "Garage sale. I paid five dollars for the box, and I should be able to sell the good ones for a couple of bucks apiece to my regulars."

"You know," I said, "I make enough off the Nibbles commercials I could be paying you for mine."

He tousled my hair affectionately. "You're my daughter, Junior. You don't need to pay me."

I hugged him tightly. "Much grass, Senior," I told him. "You da man."

"Hey, speaking of money, do you need some cash?"

I considered the question. I was now halfway through my free first week at the Roomy Toilet. If I was going to be staying on, I'd need to pay Mrs. Smedleigh a hundred bucks on Friday the eighth, only four days away. I still had about eighty-five dollars of the hundred Morty had started me out with, maybe a hundred and thirty, counting my own money.

The point of this emancipation business, though—at least *legally*—was that I was supposed to be making it on my own, without help from the 'rents. Sure, the whole thing was a stunt, but I'm pretty stubborn once I get an idea in my head, and I wanted to see if I really *could* be responsible for myself, while it lasted.

So I freed myself from the hug and tousled *his* thinning coiffure. "Thanks, Pops," I said, "but I'm good."

There were two empty chairs at dinner that evening and bowls of some strange reddish-orange goop on the table.

"What's *that* stuff?" I asked Mrs. Smedleigh, as she dished a pretty pink salmon filet onto my plate.

"That's mango salsa, dear. For the fish."

"Fish with salsa? I'm sorry, but *eeuw*?"

Jeff reached out and pushed one of the bowls towards me. "You should try it," he said. "We had it last month, and it was dynamite. Even the picky Ms. Justice broke down and had some."

"Mind your own eating habits," Libby said crossly. "But it *was* tasty, June. Just take a little bit of it and see what you think."

So I spooned a smidgeon of salsa onto my fish, and to my surprise, it was delicious! Who'da thunk it? I ladled on some more, and Moonchild pointed across the table at me, at what I was doing, and then at himself. "June, spoon, Moon," he said solemnly.

"Goon," I laughed, and dug in.

"Where are Dr. Le Groth and Mr. Marlowe?" Miss Roberts inquired.

"The doc was at a seminar today," I said. "Isn't he back?"

"Yes, dear," said Mrs. Smedleigh, "he's in his room. He returned late this afternoon and said he wasn't feeling well. And Phillip should be down any moment. I think he was in the shower."

As if on cue, there was a clattering on the stairs, and Phil burst into the dining room, his hair still wet and unbrushed.

"My watch!" he spluttered. "Which one of you dirty—?"

"*Mr.* Marlowe," Miss Roberts cut him off, "calm yourself. What has happened?"

"I was just in the shower," he said, "and I left my Rolex on my dresser with my keys and wallet. Then, when I got back to my room—my wallet and keys were still there, but my watch was gone!"

The dining room went dead silent. This was bad. Dr. Le Groth's radio wasn't worth much, and Fido's bowl wasn't worth *anything*—but even I knew that a Rolex was a top-of-the-line timepiece and cost a bundle. All at once, the situation had turned serious.

"I didn't go into your room, Phil," said Libby softly.

"I know that, Lib. It's not you I'm thinking about." And he glared pointedly at Jeff Montague.

"Hey, don't look at *me*," Jeff protested. "I wasn't in your room, either, and I didn't take your watch."

"So you claim," said Phil, his voice dangerously level.

"This is getting *way* out of hand," I said. "Isn't it time we call the police?"

"Surely that's not necessary?" Miss Roberts scoffed.

"No, I think June is right," said Mrs. Smedleigh. "I simply can *not* have this horrid nonsense happening in my home."

And then the oddest thing happened.

Phil Marlowe's head twitched as if he was shaking off a punch. "Oh, my gosh," he said slowly. "I just realized—I am *so* sorry, Jeff, I totally forgot."

Jeff's brow furrowed. "What are you talking about?"

"It's just—I'm so used to putting my things in their proper places, I completely forgot I dropped my watch off at the jeweler's this afternoon to have it cleaned. It wasn't stolen, it's in the shop!"

The tension broke, and we all laughed the incident off, but something about Phil's attitude didn't ring true to me. His watch really *had* been stolen, I felt sure of it—but, for some reason, he didn't want the cops brought in.

Why? What in the world was he trying to hide?

* * *

After dinner, I was on my way up to my room when my cell phone vibrated in my pocket. I paused on the third-floor landing to take the call and saw Morty's name on the screen.

I tapped the green button and resumed climbing. "Secret Agent Man!"

"Not so secret, Chickie, I'm in the book. So how's by you?"

"I'll tell you what's secret," I said. "My career. Where's all the publicity this dopey stunt of yours was supposed to get me?"

"Give it *time*, dolling. You've been emancipated for, what, three days? These things don't heppen overnight. I'm working on it, trust me."

"Yeah, sure. I—"

"But speaking of your career, that's eckshally why I'm calling. I just got off the phone with Sylvia Akers—it's last minute, I know, but Yummy Nibbles decided they need a new spot for summer, and Sid and Sylvia want to shoot it tomorrow. You can make it, dolling?"

"Oh, gee, Morty, I was planning on going to Europe tomorrow."

"I'm sorry, Chickie, she just this second called me. You want I should ring her back and cancel?"

"No, no, it's fine. Actually, it's funny, I was just saying to somebody this morning that I didn't know *when* the next one was coming up."

"Now you know, dolling! I'll pick you up at eight-thirty?"

"I'll be ready!"

I hung up and set my phone on my night table, hopped onto the bed, scooped up Bennington, and held him on my lap, facing me.

"Remember the Berenstain Bears?" I asked him. "*The Bear Detectives and the Case of the Missing Pumpkin?* Why can't *you* be a crime solver, Benny, like Brother and Sister Bear?"

Bennington stared at me sympathetically but didn't reply.

"I have no idea what's going on with Fido's bowl," I said, "but first Dr. Le Groth's radio went missing, and now Phil's watch either did or didn't—and last night the two of them were up to something mysterious in the doctor's room. Can't you just figure this all out and explain it to me?"

Bennington remained silent.

"I'm fourteen years old, and I'm talking to a stuffed animal," I said. "This has got to stop."

I hugged my bear, kissed his worn-out little nose, and set him back in his place, then picked up my Sudoku book, just for something to carry—never underestimate the power of props!—and headed down to the third floor to see what I could find out from Dr. Le Groth himself.

I made it all the way to his door and had my fist raised to knock when I realized I had no idea what to *say* to him. There were important questions I wanted to ask—Why had Phil gone to see him late last night? Why wasn't he listed anywhere on the internet?—but how was I supposed to ask them without tipping my hand and revealing what I was up to?

How did the Bear Detectives do it? How did Nate the Great and the BloodHounds do it? In their storybooks, they all just went right out there and *investigated*. But here I was, blundering around in the dark without the vaguest sense of where I was going or how to get there.

Oh, well, I thought. *The only way to do it is to* do it.

I gritted my teeth and knocked—and the door swung open to reveal Dr. Le Groth sitting on the edge of his bed in striped pajamas, stashing something beneath his pillow. He looked up guiltily.

"Sorry," I said. "I guess the door wasn't closed all the way."

"Yes, I—it's all right, June. What can I do for you?"

I took a quick look around the room. Like Phil's, like Moonchild's, it was pretty generic: bed, dresser, desk, chair. Was I the only one there who'd hung stuff on the walls and tried to turn my hundred and fifty square feet of boarding-house space into something resembling a home?

"Is it okay if I come in?"

He put a fist to his mouth and coughed. "In fact, I'm feeling rather ill. Perhaps another time."

I grabbed at that opening. "Yeah, Mrs. Smedleigh said you were sick. That's why I knocked. I just wanted to see if you needed anything."

He closed his eyes and rubbed his eyelids with a thumb and forefinger. "That's very thoughtful of you, June. I believe I just need to get a good night's sleep, though. So if you'll excuse me, I—"

"Did you hear about Phil's watch?" I said quickly, trying to keep the conversation going at least a little longer.

He opened his eyes in apparent surprise. "Not another theft, surely?"

"Well, he thought so, at first. He was all accusing everybody—except Libby, I think he's kind of into her—but then I said we ought to call the police, and he suddenly remembered he took it to the shop to get fixed or something."

"My goodness, I certainly missed an exciting dinner." He rose ponderously to his feet and came over to the door and put his hand on it. "I trust the meal was up to our landlady's usual high standard?"

"Yeah, it was great: salmon with this mango salsa on it. I never had it before, but it was—"

"You'll tell me all about it in the morning," he said, cutting me off. "Right now, though, June, I really must get some sleep. You understand, I'm sure."

"Sure, I—"

But he gently pushed the door closed, and this time, I could hear the latch click into place.

In the parlor, Miss Roberts was in her usual spot, stitching away with grim determination. What would happen when she finished working her way through the Ten Commandments, I wondered. Would she go back to the beginning and start over, make up an eleventh, or move on to something else altogether?

Moonchild and Jeff were in two of the three upholstered chairs, trying to hold a conversation, and Libby and Phil were sitting side by side on the couch, playing Boggle.

"June, come join us!" called Libby.

"I don't mind Boggling," I said.

"That's mind-boggling, man," Moonchild giggled.

Phil broke up laughing. "You're on a roll tonight, Moonman. You want to play?"

"No, man, I'm cool."

"I'll play," Jeff said and swung his chair around to face the couch while I moved the vacant one.

"Great," Phil murmured, but he didn't sound like he meant it.

"Come on, Moonchild," I pleaded, "don't just sit there by yourself. You, too, Miss Roberts, don't you want to play?"

"Certainly not," the spinster said, not even looking up from her handwork.

Moonchild came over and sat on the edge of the couch closest to Libby. "I'll watch," he said. "My mind's already boggled enough, man."

I took a piece of typing paper from the pile on the coffee table, folded it in half, and arranged my Sudoku book on my knee and the paper on top of the book. There were pens on the table, too, and when Jeff and I were all set, Phil picked up the game tray, settled the translucent blue plastic cover in place, and shook it violently.

"Tsk," Miss Roberts huffed.

Phil set the tray down on the coffee table and removed the cover, and Libby reversed the little hourglass and said, "Go!"

I studied the sixteen lettered cubes arranged in a four-by-four square for a moment and then began to scribble furiously on my paper.

EAT

TEA

ATE….

"Time," Libby announced, three minutes later, when the sand had finished spilling into the bottom half of the hourglass. "June, you want to start?"

"Do I have to go first?"

"I'll start," Jeff offered and began reading out his list of words.

"TON," he said, and Libby, Phil, and I chorused, "Got it!"

We all crossed it off our lists, and Jeff continued: "NOT, NOTE, NOTES, TONE, TONES, TIC—"

"Can you *please* say all your three-letter words first," Libby complained, "and *then* go on to your four-letters?"

Jeff pursed his lips. "Sure," he said, "no problem. CAT, TAC—"

"Is that three letters or four?"

"Three letters: T-A-C."

Libby shook her head. "Not a word."

"Of course, it's a word. As in TIC TAC TOE."

"I'm pretty sure it's legit," I said. "I can't believe I didn't see it."

"Thank you, Miss Knight," Jeff said with a courtly bow. "Where was I? TIP, PIT, LIT, ZIT—"

"ZIT?"

"Libby looked in the mirror," Jeff teased, "and squeezed a big honking ZIT."

"You—" Libby spluttered. "You—"

"Did you guys ever notice," I said, trying to defuse the situation, "that there's only two F's and one K, and they're all on the same die, so you can't spell—"

Miss Roberts must have been eavesdropping, because she jumped to her feet and said, "*You* have a filthy mouth, young lady! In my day, we would have washed it out with soap."

"I didn't say it," I protested. "I wasn't *going* to *say* it!"

"I don't intend to sit here and listen to this—this disgusting—"

She gathered her things together and marched out of the room.

I looked around at the rest of them and grimaced. "I *wasn't* going to say it."

Moonchild was leaning forward, studying the sixteen lettered dice in the tray. "How do you even *know* that, man?"

"My friends and I figured it out one time. We were playing Dirty Boggle—you get bonus points for swears and body parts—but nobody ever got that one, so we checked. They must have set up the letters on purpose so nobody'd be able to spell it."

"Dirty Boogie Boggle," Jeff mused. "I like it. Too bad you can't spell—"

"Coffee, anyone?" said Mrs. Smedleigh, leaning in through the French doors.

"Yeah, that, either. No, thanks, Mrs. S! But, actually, I was about to say—"

"Don't even go there," Libby whispered fiercely, as the landlady disappeared again. "I'll wash *your* mouth out with soap."

"FORK," Jeff protested. "I was gonna say FORK!"

"Of course you were."

And we resumed counting.

Jeff and Phil both had IRIS, but I was the only one who saw IRISES, which got me three points.

"How did I miss IRIS and IRISES?" Libby complained. "Mrs. Smedleigh has dozens of them out front!"

"You know all her plants and flowers come from some painter's garden in Givenchy," Jeff said. "Manet, I think."

"It's *Monet*, not *Manet*," said Libby. "Claude Monet. And Givenchy was a dress designer. Monet's garden was in *Giverny*."

"It's French," Phil said with a wink.

We played for almost an hour and finally packed it in around ten, when Jeff hit five hundred points. Libby and Phil were both in the three hundreds, and I brought up the rear with one eighty-five. I felt sort of dumb to be that far behind, but, hey, emancipated or not, I'm still just a kid.

* * *

I never sleep well, the night before a shoot. Jitters, I guess. At midnight, I was still wide awake—I tried reading, but I just couldn't concentrate: I kept focusing in on one word and trying to anagram it.

I finally decided to bang my head against a couple of Sudokus, but I couldn't find the book. I was about to run downstairs screaming out the news of another theft when I remembered I'd left it on the coffee table with my Boggle score. So I *slunk* downstairs, *not* screaming, in the dim illumination of the nightlights on the third- and second-floor landings.

The dining room and parlor were dark, but a faint glow came from the back of the house. Was someone in the kitchen? Tiptoeing gingerly so as not to wake Mrs. Smedleigh, I crossed the dining room and went through the arch.

The refrigerator door was open, and a slim figure was silhouetted against it. Not tall enough to be Mrs. S, too thin for Miss Roberts.

"Hi, Libby," I whispered, and the figure whirled around, startled by the sound.

"June?" she said softly.

"You can't sleep, either?"

"No, I—I was thirsty. I thought I'd get a glass of milk. You want one?"

"No, thanks. I just came down to get my book and saw the light."

"I'm getting a little scared," she said. "Nobody's really talking about it, but we still don't know who stole Dr. Le Groth's radio." She took the jug from the fridge and left the door open while she got down a glass and poured. "Do you have any idea who it might have been?"

"I've been trying to figure it out. I mean, nothing like that ever happened until Phil and I moved in, so I guess I understand the doctor thinking it must have been one of us."

"I never believed for a second it was you, June. And I—I've gotten to know Phil a little, and I don't think he did it, either."

"And it wasn't *you*," I said. I didn't *want* it to be her—but then I didn't want it to be *any* of them, not even Miss Roberts and her bar of soap. "*Somebody* did it, though. I mean, you can't just *lose* a clock radio. And what about Fido's bowl?"

And Phil's watch, I wanted to add, but she was obviously sweet on him, and I didn't want to say anything to put her on the defensive.

"So it pretty much had to have been Miss Roberts or Moonchild," Libby said.

"Or Jeff."

She shook her head. "Jeff and I don't get along, but I work with him every day. I've known him since junior high. He's not a thief."

"If it has to be *one* of them," I said, "and I guess it does, then I'm sort of leaning towards Moonchild."

"That poor man? But *why*, June?"

"Well, he's the only one I can think of who might have had a motive."

"What motive?"

"Money. Everybody else has a job, except Miss Roberts, and she's got her retirement. Maybe Moonchild stole the radio and hocked it to get some extra cash."

"But what about Fido's bowl?" she said, swinging the refrigerator door closed, which plunged the room into near-darkness, the only illumination coming from a weak bulb set just outside the still-open sliding glass door to the back yard.

"I don't know," I said. "That part doesn't make any sense at all."

Picking my way carefully through the quiet house, I found my puzzle book where I'd left it on the coffee table and slipped silently back up to my room.

June's Log: June 5

I must have fallen asleep, finally, because I remember waking up about five-thirty. I stayed in bed till six, but then I couldn't stand it anymore and crept downstairs with a book, unlocked the front door, and let myself out onto the porch.

I tried the swing gingerly and found, to my surprise, that it had been well oiled and didn't creak, so I settled back and opened my well-worn copy of *Perks of Being a Wallflower*. I've read it about a million times, but it's one of those books I can read over and over again and always find something new.

Around page forty, I heard the front door open and looked up to see Moonchild in a baggy Hawaiian shirt and tattered gym shorts, a white bath towel slung over his shoulder, a Super Bowl XL ballcap on his head.

"Hey, man, you're up early," he said. "Mind if I join you?"

That was an interesting question. If he was, in fact, the Roomy Toilet's radio thief, I sort of *did* mind him sharing the swing with me. On the other hand, maybe a little one-on-one conversation might lead him into making a damaging admission.

So I scooted over to make room for him, and he eased himself onto the wood-slatted seat beside me.

"You're up pretty early yourself," I said, closing the book and setting it down between us.

"I always come out around this time for a smoke," he said, fishing a Ziploc baggie, a little pack of rolling papers, and a cheap plastic lighter out of his voluminous shirt pocket. "Mrs. S would *kill* me if I lit up in the house."

Oh...my...God, I thought. I had never seen pot IRL before, just in movies, and now I was about to get a contact high or something!

He pulled a paper out of the pack, sprinkled it with tiny leaves from the baggie, licked the edge of the paper, did some sort of magical twirling motion I couldn't really see clearly, and stuck the result in his mouth.

"I—" I said.

He snapped the lighter, touched the flame to the end of the joint, and inhaled deeply. Then he sighed out the smoke and tacked a satisfied "Yeah!" at the end of the exhalation.

I was scared and fascinated at the same time. More fascinated than scared, really. And maybe this *did* help to clarify things. The more I thought about it, the more likely it seemed to me that Moonchild had been behind at *least* the theft of Dr. Le Groth's radio. I still couldn't figure out what he'd wanted with Fido's bowl, and the disappearance or *non*-disappearance of Phil's watch was a mystery I couldn't yet even begin to explain. But if Moonchild didn't just look and sound like a stoner but actually *was* one, well, that was a crime right there—and it didn't take much imagination to make the leap from seeing him using illegal drugs to envisioning him doing other illegal stuff, like stealing.

And then I noticed the smell, and it was the same acrid stink I remembered from the cigarettes my Pops used to smoke before Mom finally nagged him into quitting one New Year's.

"That—that's not grass, is it?" I said.

He held it close to his face and peered at it curiously. "Grass?" he repeated. "Whoa, Mrs. S would *really* tear me a new one if I toked up on her property! No, man, this is just regular tobacco."

I sighed, half with relief and half disappointment.

"It's cheaper to roll 'em myself than to buy 'em ready-made," he explained.

That made sense, I guess. And it opened the door to a line of questioning that might turn out to be productive.

"How much do you figure you save this way?" I asked.

"Hmm." He took another hit while he considered the math. "Last time I *bought* a pack of smokes, I paid, like, maybe five bucks, so that's, what, a quarter a cigarette? I can buy a pound of tobacco for like sixteen dollars, and that makes maybe five hundred cigarettes, plus the papers— I don't know, man, it probably costs me a couple of cents apiece to roll my own."

"That's a pretty decent savings."

"Hey, every little bit helps, you know?"

"Is money a problem?" I said craftily.

He took another drag. "Not for *me*, man. I'm not rich, you know, but I collect my disability every month, and that's enough to get me through."

Okay, fine, so *cherchez*'ing the money hadn't gotten me anything useful.

I decided to try a more direct approach, maybe catch him off guard.

"You have any idea who swiped Dr. Le Groth's radio, Moonchild?"

He turned toward me and studied me closely.

"I've been thinking probably *you* jacked it, man."

"*Me*? Why would I—?"

"I don't know. Why would *anybody*? Kids do stupid stuff sometimes— I know I pulled all kinds of crazy stunts when I was your age."

I'm not sure why, but for some reason, I decided to confide in him. "I've been thinking it was probably *you*," I said.

He nodded slowly. "Yeah, I bet most of 'em figure it was me. The way I look and all—you almost *gotta* peg me as the bad guy."

"But you really didn't do it?"

"Nope. I tell you what, I hope it was Miss Roberts. That old girl is *mean.*"

"Nobody's ever going to vote her Miss Congeniality," I agreed.

"A' course, if I *did* do it, I'd *say* I didn't, right? So maybe it *was* me, after all, and I'm just messin' with you."

I squinted at him. "Are you *sure* that's just tobacco in that thing?"

We sat there for a minute, Moonchild smoking, me trying to reconcile the pleasant man beside me with the drug-addled criminal I'd just about had him pigeonholed as. I had hoped that a conversation with the aging hippie would result in a slip that would confirm my suspicions of him, but in fact, I found myself *less* sure of his guilt than I'd been before we started talking.

If "con-" is the opposite of "pro-," then what's the opposite of "progress"?

Apparently, it was whatever *I* was making….

Somewhere along the line, one of us had started the swing moving lazily back and forth. It might have been me, but I hadn't noticed myself doing it.

It was nice, sitting there on the porch swinging with Moonchild, and I leaned back and let myself enjoy it.

After a while, just for something to break the silence, I asked him, "What's the towel for?"

"For her," he said, pointing the last remaining inch of his cigarette down the street. In the distance, a woman had just turned the corner of Chatman Drive and was jogging towards us. Moonchild licked his thumb and forefinger and squeezed the burning end of his cigarette butt. It went out with a soft hiss, and he dropped it into his baggie, zipped it shut, and stashed it away in his pocket.

Libby Justice turned up the walk and ran to the foot of the porch steps, then dropped to the ground and did some stretches. She was wearing black Spandex stretch pants and an oversized Race for the Cure T-shirt with the sleeves cut off over a gray sports bra, and her long strawberry-blond hair was held back by a terrycloth headband that featured the same Nike swoosh that was on her white running shoes. Her forehead glistened with a sheen of sweat, and she was breathing heavily.

When she finished stretching out her muscles, Moonchild threw the towel to her, and she came up the porch steps, mopping her face and armpits.

"You run often?" I asked.

"Every morning," she panted. "Four miles, rain or shine."

"You must really enjoy it."

"I hate every minute of it," she laughed, her breathing beginning to slow. "But I love it, too. What do they say, 'hate the sin, love the sinner'?"

Moonchild nodded sagely. "That's deep," he said. And then he narrowed his eyes and added, "Like, what does it mean?"

Libby threw the towel at him. "I have no idea," she said. "Thanks, buddy. I'm gonna hit the shower. I'll see you two at breakfast." And she went inside.

I wasn't too worried about what I wore today, since they'd be dressing me for success at the shoot. So I threw on a pair of cargo shorts and a hoodie and my lucky dangly earrings with the mask of comedy on one side and tragedy on the other, slipped into my favorite flip-flops, and was in the dining room at the stroke of seven-thirty. A grim-faced Jeff was already working his way through a cheese omelet and a toasted English muffin, Miss Roberts was picking at hers fussily, and Moonchild, hunched forward with his elbows on the table and his shaggy head in his hands, hadn't even touched his.

"I got ripped off, man," he howled as soon as he saw me.

"No way," I said, shocked. "What did they take?"

"My leather vest! You know, with all the fringe on it?"

"That's awful! Was it still there when you woke up this morning, before you went out on the porch?"

"Oh, man, *I* don't know. I just know I went upstairs to get it, and it was *gone.*"

Phil and Libby came in together. There was a knife-edge crease in his black slacks, and his blue-and-green-striped shirt was perfectly pressed. Libby's hair was frizzier than usual. She had on a sheer white blouse with a ruffled collar over a matching white camisole and a royal-blue A-line skirt sprinkled with tiny white stars.

"Is today the Fifth of June or the Fourth of July?" Jeff said in a stage whisper as Phil held her chair for her. "I feel like I ought to salute."

"Very amusing," Libby said coldly—but with her frizzy red hair, white blouse, and star-spangled blue skirt, she *did* look kind of like an American flag. "I'm in no mood for your juvenile sense of humor," she said. "Now *I've* been robbed."

"You, too?" I said. "Somebody took Moonchild's leather vest."

"And my hair dryer. It was brand-new—I just bought it a week ago."

"I've had that vest since Woodstock," Moonchild said mournfully.

Jeff looked up from his omelet. "You can't possibly have been at Woodstock," he said, his voice clearly skeptical. "You weren't even—"

"Not Woodstock One, man. Woodstock *Two,* in '94. When they had the first one in—what was it, '69?—I wasn't even *born* yet."

"They had fringed leather vests at Woodstock Two, Moonchild?" Libby asked.

"*I* had one! And now it's gone, man. This is *bogus!* You don't rip off a dude's *vest,* man—that's *wrong.*"

"And why in the world would somebody take my hair dryer?" Libby demanded. "It cost me ten dollars at Target." She pointed an accusing finger at Jeff. "If this is your idea of a joke—"

"Don't be insulting," Jeff snapped.

"I wonder about you, Montague," said Phil. "You've been pestering Libby since the day I got here."

"What is your problem, *Marlowe*? Everything was just fine and dandy before *you* moved in."

"I'd like to know what's happened to 'Dr.' Le Groth," Miss Roberts said prissily, her index and middle fingers making very definite air quotes. "He seems to have disappeared. Perhaps he's absconded with his loot?"

"With a cat's bowl, an old vest, and a hairdryer?"

"And, like, his own radio?" Moonchild added.

"I don't think these thefts have anything to do with the value of the items stolen," the spinster said. "There's something else going on here, something—*pagan*."

"He was in his room last night," I said. "I talked with him. He said he wasn't feeling well. He's probably just sleeping late."

Mrs. Smedleigh came in with more omelets, and we brought her up to date on the latest thefts. She was scandalized, of course, but she didn't have any better idea what to do about it than the rest of us.

Our crime spree seemed to be gathering speed. After the first theft on Sunday (Dr. Le Groth's radio), the rest of the Breakfast Bunch were in agreement there'd been one additional incident on Monday (Fido's bowl)—although I still found myself thinking that Phil's watch had been stolen, too, despite his "remembering" he'd taken it to the shop. Either way, here it was Tuesday. There'd already been two more thefts today, and it wasn't even nine in the morning yet.

Phil made a quick note in his little book, and a car horn sounded from out in the street. "That's my ride," I said. "See you later, everyone!"

I crammed a quick bite of omelet in my mouth, snatched a slice of buttered wheat toast, and took off.

Morty was parked in the driveway in his gleaming silver PT Cruiser. It was a beautiful day, he had the moonroof open, and his bald head was glistening in the sunlight. He had on his usual professional get-up—a natty tan linen suit, polka-dot tie, and brown loafers with little tassels on them—and he was wearing aviator shades, which made him look younger than his sixty-some years.

"Ready for ection, Chickie?" he greeted me.

"Ready, willing, and able," I replied, as I always did when he picked me up for a shoot.

"Then let's get this show on the road!"

The Yummy Nibbles Company is a division of the National Pet Foods Corporation, which is a wholly owned subsidiary of Amalgamated Comestibles, which is the US arm of Wohlschmeckend Produkten GmBH, itself the German branch of Al-Areen Enterprises, a Kuwaiti holding company. Yummy Nibbles has somehow managed to maintain a large measure of independence from its parent and grandparent and great-grandparent and great-great-grandparent companies, and all of its advertising is still produced right here in town by Akers & Akers, a husband-and-wife outfit operating out of a funky old Nineteenth Century fire station in the Warehouse District.

Mrs. Akers "discovered" me eight years ago, when I played Gretl, the youngest of the Trapp Family Singers, and her son Lippy played Rolfe in our unified school district's production of *The Sound of Music*. I was in the first grade—it wasn't until I finished elementary school that Mom and Pops decided to home-school me—and Lippy was a junior in high school. I have no idea what was up with the nickname—his lips seemed perfectly normal to me—but that was what everyone called him. He was even listed as Lippy Akers in the program.

Anyway, Mrs. Akers liked what she saw of me on stage and invited me down to the fire station for a screen test. She showed the tape to the folks at Yummy Nibbles, they liked what *they* saw, and I've been the Yummy Nibbles spokeskid ever since.

I make a new commercial about every three months, and they're all frankly variations on the same basic theme. I'm out somewhere being a kid—at a playground, an amusement park, the zoo, the mall—and I see some other youngster (always a new actor, used for one spot only) having trouble getting his (or her) dog to eat the food he (or she) has set down in front of it. I reach into the backpack I conveniently happen to be carrying around town with me, pull out a bag (or box, or can) of the sponsor's finest, and say, with great enthusiasm, "Here, why not try Yummy Nibbles, the dog food dogs love more than people love people food!" Dog snarfs down product, interchangeable Second Child gushes thanks, I hold up the bag/box/can to the camera, beam winningly, and say, "Why don't *you* pick up some Yummy Nibbles for *your* little friend, *today*!" And scene.

This time around, we were filming in front of a photorealistic backdrop of a beach. It probably would have been easier just to *go* to the beach, but Akers & Akers is still using those old-fashioned pedestal TV cameras that have to be cabled to both an electric power supply and a three-quarter-inch video recorder, so it's tough for them to go out on location. Instead, they'd rented the backdrop from a theatrical-supply house way out in Chicago and trucked in about a zillion pounds of sand, and the script had me walking along the "beach" in a cute little two-piece swimsuit I never in a million years would have thought to pick out for myself, licking a cherry Popsicle as I walked, my backpack incongruously slung over one shoulder.

And there beside a half-constructed sand castle would be— surprise!—some perky little Munchkin, ranging in age from three or four to eight or nine years old, trying to coerce some frisky little dog to dig into a bowl of the Other Brand.

When Morty and I arrived at the converted fire station, director Garrison Stasheff introduced us to the Munchkin *du jour* (a six-year-old towheaded boy named Mikey), the dog *du jour* (a two-year-old Bichon

Frise named Larchmont), and Larchmont's handlers, a flamboyant couple named Danny and Manny who had my gaydar pinging from twenty paces off. After shaking hands and paws all around, I pulled my agent off to the side of the bustling studio for a heart-to-heart conversation.

"Listen, Morty," I said, "I am totally going to need some more money by the end of this week. I've got rent due on Friday."

"Already? What heppened to the hundred smackers I fronted you the other day?"

"I still have most of it," I said, "but the rent at the Roomy Toilet is a hundred a week, and I—"

"The rent at the excuse me?"

I explained about Dylan and Carson and the sign, and Morty chuckled. "The Roomy Toilet! That's a good one! So you're living in a toilet but you're not exactly flush, is that the story?"

I groaned. "That's terrible," I said.

"Anyway," he went on, "what are you talking? You must have *thousands* in your savings by now."

I shook my head. "That's my college fund, Morty, you know that. And, anyway, it's a trust account—I can't make a withdrawal without Mom or Pops' signature, and I don't want to ask them for help. I'm supposed to be doing this *without* them, remember?"

He patted my shoulder approvingly. "You're taking this whole thing seriously, Chickie, I like that. So, fine, I'll drop in on Sid and Sylvia Akers this efternoon and see if I can get you an advance against your next check."

"You're not sticking around for the shoot?"

"Not this time, Chickie. I got places to go and people to see. And tonight I got, you should excuse the expression, a date."

"Seriously? That's great, Morty! Who's the lucky lady?"

"I'm not exectly ready to tell you about her yet, dolling, I don't want

I should jinx the whole relationship. But this much I'll give you as a coming attraction: she's a wonderful lady, and I got high-epple-pie-in-the-sky hopes for the situation."

I grimaced. "Inappropriate," I said. Then, reconsidering: "On the other hand, who says you can't teach an old dog new tricks?"

He glanced over at Danny and Manny, who were on their knees next to Larchmont, fussing over the little snowball's plumed tail, each of them with a comb and a hairbrush.

"Sometimes, it's the *new* dog that's hard to teach," he said. "I wish you and Gary luck. That bitch is nothing but trouble."

"Um, actually, Morty, I think Larchmont's a boy."

"That may well be true, Chickie, but I represent him, and I'm telling you, he's a bitch to work with. You'll see."

"Thanks for the warning," I said. "Hey, if you're taking off, how am I supposed to get back to Smedley Street? It's a long walk from—"

"Don't worry, Houston, we got no problem. I already talked with Gary: he'll drop you off when you're finished here."

"You're the best, Morty. And if the Akers come through with an advance, *you*'ll drop some cash off at the house?"

"Ebsalutely! I'll stop by before my date, take a good look at this Roomy Toilet you're living in."

He turned to go, then swung back and cried out, "Have fun storming de kestle!" in a surprisingly good impression of Billy Crystal as Miracle Max in *The Princess Bride*.

First a date, and now this? Good old Morty, always random, always full of surprises.

By the time the crew had the set dressed and lit and the camera positions taped off, it was close to eleven. Meanwhile, Danny and Manny worked with Larchmont while Gary ran Mike the Munchkin and me through a couple of rehearsals.

Gary grew up in the Midwest, went East to attend film school at NYU, then worked his way up from gopher to production assistant to assistant director at one of the networks. After six years in the business, he was offered a shot directing a daily soap opera. "When you go into this racket," he told me, the first time we met, "they give you a stopwatch and an ulcer. Later, when you retire, you have to give back the stopwatch—but they let you keep the ulcer."

With that cautionary tale in mind, Gary ultimately decided to turn down the soap and found a less stressful gig making thirty-second spots for Akers & Akers.

He was good at what he did, he ran a relaxed set, and he was fun to work for.

Today, though, we might as well have been in New York.

Larchmont, it turned out, really *was* a bitch to work with—Morty the Agent is never wrong about a client!—and the shoot took way longer than expected. Someone apparently forgot to explain to the fluffy little puffball, who seemed to have approximately the same intelligence level as your average avocado, that the Other Brand is supposed to be nasty. In take after take after take, he dove into his bowl of Other Brandies with gusto and practically bit the Munchkin's hand off when Mikey tried to pull it away from him.

After the tenth try, Larchmont was so full Danny and Manny had to carry him out to the alley behind the building and make him throw up before we could continue.

While the three of them were being gross out back, I wandered over to the snack table for something other than a Popsicle. There was a big plate of Girl Scout cookies, a bowl of fruit, thermoses of coffee and decaf, and a dozen cans of soda in assorted flavors. I debated treating myself to a Samoa, but the little voice in the back of my head said *Enough already with the sugar, dolling,* and I nibbled half a banana instead.

As I stood there trying to decide whether to throw the other half away, put it back in the bowl, or force myself to eat it, Mikey came up and began stuffing his face with Do-Si-Dos and his pockets with Trefoils.

"You don't have to steal them," I said. "They're free."

He looked up at me, his mouth ringed with chocolate, and—looking for all the world like a miniature Dustin Hoffman—mumbled, "If they're free, then I'm not stealing them, am I?"

He had a point. I threw the rest of my banana in the trash and went back to the set.

Even after barfing, all the stupid dog would do was carry on gobbling OBs the moment Mikey set the bowl in front of him. We never once got *close* to the point where I was supposed to say my line.

By four-thirty, Gary'd already had to send out twice for more Popsicles, and I was beginning to really *hate* the taste of cherry.

"We need to switch to a different dog," I suggested.

"Not an option," said Gary. "We have to get this thing in the can *today*."

"Can we at least switch to a different flavor Popsicle?" I begged.

"Sorry, kiddo, we need the red for color balance."

I sighed.

"All right, everyone, let's do it again!" Gary yelled wearily and headed back to the control room.

I moved over to my mark, and Gillian the makeup girl touched up my hair while Danny and Manny did the same for Larchmont's coat.

"Thirty seconds," the floor manager yelled. "Quiet, please!"

Gillian whispered, "Knock 'em dead, June!" and scurried out of camera range, and the studio fell silent, except for Larchmont's panting.

The floor manager held up a hand. "Five, four, three, two, one," he counted and then punched his index finger at me. I started whistling the Yummy Nibble's jingle and walking. The red light on top of Camera One winked on, and we were rolling.

Walk walk walk, whistle whistle whistle, blah blah blah, and there's the sand castle and Mikey pushing Larchmont's nose into the bowl of Other Brandies and urging, "Please, boy, you have to eat! It's *good* for you!"

For a moment, the adorable little snowball hesitated.

Come on, Larchie, I thought. *Don't eat that awful stuff, it's* bad *for you. Come on, boy, Upward Facing Dog!*

But Larchmont shook off his hesitation as if he'd just stepped out of the ocean and was shaking off ten gallons of salt water and moved smoothly into Greedily Gobbling Dog, and Gary yelled, "Cut it!" so loudly I could hear his angry voice leak through the floor manager's headphones.

After thirty-two spoiled takes, I finally suggested putting Yummy Nibbles in Larchmont's bowl and the Other Brand in the Yummy Nibbles bag.

"That'll never work," Manny frowned. "This dratted dog will eat *anything.*"

"It can't hurt to try it, sweetie," said Danny.

"Fine," Manny huffed. "What's one more take?"

"It's not exactly ethical," Gary said, "but we have to get this thing *shot.* Let's give it a whirl."

So we did. And Take Thirty-Three, of course, went off smooth as silk. Larchmont turned up his wet little nose at the bowl of Yummy Nibbles masquerading as Other Brandies, then yipped happily and dug right into the Other Brandies masquerading as Yummy Nibbles the instant I set them in front of him.

"Print it!" Gary announced with unconcealed relief. "That's a wrap, people, thanks!"

When we left the studio, Gary took me and the crew out for pizza and beer. (Well, Diet Coke with lime for me, although Gillian let me take a sip of her Pilsner Urquell—and one sip was plenty. I don't know how grownups *drink* that stuff!)

By the time he dropped me back at the Roomy Toilet, it was after seven. As I came up the porch steps, the front door opened, and Libby and Phil came out, chattering animatedly.

"Where are you two off to?" I asked.

"We're going to see a movie," Libby said.

"Oh, cool. Which one?"

"No idea. We're just going to head up to the mall and see what's playing. How'd your commercial go?"

"It was grueling, don't even ask. How was dinner?"

Phil grimaced. "That was pretty grueling, too. There's been another theft."

I gasped. "What was stolen? From who?"

"Jeff's electric razor," Libby said. "He practically came right out and accused me of taking it. That's why we decided to get out of the house for a while. It's pretty chilly in there at the moment."

"His *razor*?" The whole situation kept getting stranger. None of it was making any *sense*.

"Look on the bright side." Phil's smile was strained. "At least this clears *you*. You were away all day—you *couldn't* have taken it."

Libby shook her head. "I'm not trying to cause you any trouble, June, but I saw Jeff in the bathroom shaving this morning when I came in from my run, and you were out on the porch with Moonchild. So the fact is you could have grabbed the razor before you left for your shoot."

"Well, I didn't," I said. "What would I want with Jeff's stupid razor?"

"You don't shave your legs yet?" Phil asked.

"With an *electric* razor? I don't think so."

"Nobody's accusing you, June," Libby tried to placate me. "*I'm the one Jeff's mad at.*"

"Anyway, listen," Phil said, "we better go. Try and stay out of Jeff's way, okay, and we'll catch you later on?"

They went down the steps, and I headed into the house. As I turned to close the door behind me, I saw Phil take Libby's arm and lead her to a gleaming red Jetta parked at the curb. He opened the passenger door for her and helped her in, then leaned over to whisper something in her ear before circling around and climbing into the driver's seat. The engine roared to life, and Libby stuck a pale arm out the window and waved as the car took off down Smedley Street.

I wondered if getting away from Jeff's suspicions was the *only* reason they were going to a movie together. Actually, I doubted it. There was definitely something going on between the two of them.

"Yes, I suppose you're right, dear," Mrs. Smedleigh said. I'd found her in the kitchen, unloading the dishwasher, and she'd given me the bad news that no one had stopped by to deliver an envelope stuffed with Akers & Akers of cash for me. She'd offered to warm up some leftover lamb chops, but fortunately, I was so full of veggie pizza I wasn't even tempted. (Lamb chops? Don't they make those out of little baby sheep? I mean, that's *sick!*) Then, when I told her I'd heard about Jeff's razor from Libby and Phil and ventured my suspicion that there might be a little romance beginning to percolate between them, she nodded and agreed with me.

"I'll admit I'm a little disappointed," she went on. "I've always hoped that she and Jeffrey would patch up their differences and—well, Philip's a lovely young man. Perhaps it's just as well."

I helped her put the rest of the plates and bowls and glasses and silverware away, then drifted off when she began making a list for a grocery run.

I'd bypassed the parlor on my way in, heading straight through the dining room to the back of the house in search of Mrs. S. Libby and

Phil had made it sound like Jeff was on the warpath, and I really didn't want to get in the way of his slings and arrows. By now, though, I hoped he'd had time to calm down, and I figured I ought to get myself brought up to speed. Maybe he'd seen or heard something I could use as a clue.

So I took a deep, cleansing breath, swung open the French doors, and poked my head through the gap between them—and, to my surprise, the parlor was empty.

Libby and Phil were on their way to the mall, but where were Jeff, Moonchild, Miss Roberts, and Dr. Le Groth? Probably in their rooms, standing guard over what was left of their stuff.

On the way upstairs to fetch my laptop, I saw that Libby's door was standing half open. I went over to pull it closed, but then on a sudden impulse pushed it wide instead and stood in the hallway with my hand on the knob, looking in.

Unlike Phil, Moonchild, and the doctor, Libby had added some personal touches to her living quarters. She'd hung three cheerful framed prints that obviously hadn't been selected by Mrs. Smedleigh on the west wall and a bulletin board on the far wall, next to the window, with dozens of photographs and postcards and handwritten notes tacked to it, a collage of colorful images that echoed the vase of fresh flowers on her nightstand. The orange-and-yellow afghan hanging over the back of her recliner looked hand-crocheted—by her mother, perhaps?—and there were candles, a jewelry box, and an arrangement of perfume bottles on her dresser.

With all that to choose from, why had the thief taken her hair dryer? A piece of jewelry would have been more valuable, a perfume bottle would have been easier to conceal.

It seemed more obvious with each theft that the point wasn't the actual stolen items themselves, but the *act* of stealing them. Maybe the thief got off on invading our privacy, which seemed to be the kind of thing that might possibly motivate Miss Roberts. Or maybe it was the very risk of getting caught that provided the thrill—which probably pointed back again towards Moonchild.

Or maybe the person who was responsible for all this drama simply couldn't help it? Could the explanation be that simple? Could the radio, the bowl, the watch, the vest, and the hair dryer all have been taken by a kleptomaniac?

Puzzle pieces began to drop into place. Libby seemed almost compulsive about her daily run. Every morning, she'd told me, rain or shine—even though she hated doing it. And what if Phil wasn't afraid of the police, after all? What if he'd somehow realized or guessed that it was Libby who'd taken his watch? In that case, of course he wouldn't want the police brought in, not if he was already beginning to fall for her.

They were going to a movie. They'd be gone for hours. This was a perfect opportunity to search her room for the missing items.

I stood there, trying to convince myself to cross the threshold and settle the question once and for all. It would be so easy: just two steps forward, and I'd be in the room.

But I just couldn't do it. Snooping was snooping, no matter what the justification, and I was not going to be a snoop. If I couldn't figure this situation out in an honorable manner, then I wasn't *going* to figure it out at all.

Without any further hesitation, I pulled the door firmly shut—from the *outside*—and turned back towards the stairway.

Behind me, a door creaked open, and I froze. Had someone been in there all along, maybe hiding in the closet?

"Oh," said Jeff, and I turned back and saw him standing in his own doorway, right next to Libby's. "June. I heard Libby's door and thought maybe she was back."

"No, it's just me," I said, not sure if me being me and not Libby was a good thing or a bad thing. "She left her door open, so I closed it for her."

"Mmm. Hey, feel like coming in for a minute? I want to show you something."

He didn't seem to be foaming at the mouth, and his and Miss Roberts' were the only rooms I hadn't yet seen, so I said sure and followed him inside.

I expected the room to be as bland and characterless as Phil's, as Moonchild's, as Dr. Le Groth's. But Jeff, it turned out, had a surprise in store.

Every available surface in the room was occupied by carefully assembled and meticulously hand-painted plastic models. On the dresser and nightstand were a fleet of cars, an armada of aircraft carriers and pirate ships, a parade of rockets and tanks and monster trucks and Batmobiles. On the carpet in one corner, Frankenstein battled a tyrannosaurus rex and the Wolfman grappled with a wooly mammoth. A dozen model planes and helicopters and X-wing fighters and Starship Enterprises flew from strings attached to the ceiling.

"What do you think?" he said.

I approached the dresser to take a closer look. "You *made* all these?"

He nodded, and I wasn't sure from his expression if he was proud or embarrassed.

"This is incredible! There must be a hundred of them!"

"Nope, just sixty-eight. But I'll get to a hundred, sooner or later!"

"How long does it take to put one of these things together?"

"Well, it depends." He waved at the monsters and mammals in the corner. "Those are some of the first ones I ever did, back when I was, well, probably your age. I didn't know what I was doing then, but still, they probably took me four or five hours apiece. Something like this, though"—he touched one of the planes hanging overhead, a blue-and-silver propeller job with US military insignia on the sides, and it spun in a lazy circle—"this is a P-51D Mustang, 1:48 scale, and it probably took me about twenty-five, thirty hours all told. I just finished it last week."

There was a little worktable set up beside the closet door, covered with a precisely arranged assortment of plastic parts, lengths of thin black string, X-ACTO knives, tubes of glue, squares of sandpaper, paintbrushes, small jars of paint, tiny screwdrivers, tweezers, and a thick sheaf of detailed diagrams and instructions. "What's this one going to be?"

"If I ever get it finished," he sighed. "This is the most complicated model I've ever tackled. It's the *USS Kearsarge*, a Civil War ship, 1:96 scale. It's got three masts, with wood-grain decks and hatches and ladders and all these lifeboats with teeny little oars. I haven't even finished sorting the parts and cleaning off the flashing yet. I figure it'll take a hundred hours by the time I have it assembled and painted and fully rigged."

"Get *out!*"

"I usually spend an hour, an hour and a half before I go to bed, so I'm looking at two or three months' worth of work here."

And then I saw it, peeking out from beneath the pages of instructions.

"Mind if I take a look at these?" I said and, without waiting for an answer, picked up the pile of papers.

Underneath them was an electric hair dryer.

I didn't say anything, just looked silently at Jeff.

Was this it? Had I just solved the case?

The silence between us lengthened uncomfortably.

And then Jeff blinked and laughed. "Are you nuts, June? That's *mine*. I use it to dry the paint faster. If that was Libby's, you think I'd just leave it *out*?"

"It was covered up," I said lamely.

"I'm not using it right now. I told you, I'm still getting organized. It'll be *weeks* before I start to paint."

I dropped the sheaf of instructions back on the table. "This whole deal is totally starting to creep me out," I said.

"No kidding. I don't think I really took it seriously until it happened to *me*. I mean, the razor's nothing. I'll pick up another one for forty dollars at Kohl's. It's just the idea that—well, that one of *us* is doing this. It just seems so—"

"—so *dirty*," I supplied.

"Exactly." He laughed. "You really thought it was me?"

"I don't know *what* to think. It's got to be *somebody*."

"I know. I've been wracking my brains, trying to figure it out, but I—"

"I thought you thought it was Libby?"

He winced. "Yeah, I guess I sort of went off on her. I don't know why we have such a hard time getting along."

"I think she's really nice," I said.

"Of course she is. And she's pretty, and a terrific secretary. You put the two of us in the same room, though, and we're like roosters at a cockfight, circling around each other, trying to peck each other's eyes out."

"Does she know about—all this?" I waved a hand at the little world he was building.

"Sure, she—" He stopped mid-sentence and reconsidered. "Huh. Now that you ask, I don't know if she does or not. She's never been in here. She must have *seen* them, though, somewhere along the line when my door was open."

"You should invite her in and show her. I bet she'd be fascinated."

He sniffed. "Yeah, right. She'd just think I'm even weirder than she *already* thinks I am. No, I think you and I better just keep this our little secret."

"I don't know, Jeff. Don't you think there's *enough* secrets around here as it is?"

He regarded me thoughtfully. "Are you sure you're only fourteen years old?"

"Anyway," I said, "I don't think your models are weird. I think they're cool."

He held up a hand, palm towards me. I gave him a high five and went up to the attic for my electronics.

Back in the parlor, I set up my little cushioned nest beside the TV, plugged everything in, and checked my email. There was a sweet note from Pops, a thanks-for-the-good-work from Gary, and a bunch of dumb forwards and junk mail. Oh, and Allie and Brenna both wrote back to confirm our Half Moon coffee date for tomorrow at two. As a home-schooler, I don't get a lot of socialization. Thank goodness for A and B, my own personal sisterhood of the traveling pants (without the traveling pants).

A little while later, I was playing my six trillionth game of Candy Crush when I felt something brush against my jeans. It was Fido, curling around my leg. This was new—he never paid much attention to anyone except Mrs. Smedleigh.

"Hey, boy," I said in that singsong voice you use for animals and babies, "how are *you* this evening?" I stroked his soft gray fur and scratched behind his ears, and he rubbed his head against my hand and burred deep in his throat.

"He likes you, dear," said Mrs. S, who was taking advantage of Dr. Le Groth's absence to polish the dark TV screen with a big orange cloth. "Would you like to feed him? I think he's hungry."

"Can I? Sure!"

"You remember where his food is, *c'est vrai?* Don't give him too much, maybe half a cup with some warm water from the tap."

"Thanks, Mrs. Smedleigh!" I called over my shoulder, already halfway across the parlor, Fido trailing behind me.

In the kitchen at the back of the house, I opened the cabinet where Mrs. S kept Fido's goodies and grabbed his new, improved yellow bowl and the ten-pound bag of dry cat food. The Oreo bag, I noticed, was empty—maybe Moonchild had finished them off the other night, when he'd gone off looking for cookies—so I crumpled it up and put it in the trash. I scooped half a cup of nuggets into the yellow bowl, added a little extra as a special treat, then held the bowl under the tap for a second and set it down on the day-old *Straight Shooter* beside the sliding glass door. To see Fido dig in, you'd've bet he'd been taking lessons from Larchmont.

And that thought reminded me of my long day at the studio, and I suddenly found myself remembering little Mikey stuffing his pockets with cookies. I slowly turned and looked back towards Fido's cabinet, where the Oreos weren't.

Was it possible that it hadn't been Moonchild who'd taken them?

I turned back to the sliding glass door. The other times I'd been in the kitchen, it had always been half open to admit a breeze.

It was closed now.

I tugged on the vertical wooden handle, and it slid open easily. It wasn't locked.

Was it *ever* locked?

I had no idea.

Was it possible the Roomy Toilet's resident thief *wasn't* a resident, after all?

That's crazy, I thought. *A radio, a cat's bowl, an old vest, a cheap hair dryer, an electric razor? What outsider would* want *any of that?*

On the other hand, what *insider* would want it?

I slid the glass door closed—and, before leaving the kitchen, I locked it.

"You found everything, dear?" Mrs. Smedleigh asked, as I re-entered the parlor.

"Sure, I—"

My cell phone vibrated. I fished it out of the cargo pocket of my shorts and saw that it was Morty calling.

"Sorry, I have to take this," I said. "It's my agent. By the way, you're out of Oreos."

"Really? I thought—well, never mind, I'll get some more tomorrow. I have to go to the store anyway."

Heading up the stairs, I tapped the magic green button on my screen.

"Ah, yes, my little chickadee," William Claude Dukinfield drawled in my ear.

"Morty," I said, "I know this is you. I have Caller ID."

"Busted," he said in his regular voice. "I got the eccent down good, though, right?"

"Yes, indeeeeeed," I matched him. "But anyone can do W.C. Fields, my bonny boy. Ah, yes!"

"Not bed," he said proudly. "I'm telling you, Chickie, you oughta be an ectress."

"Yeah, right," I said, opening my door and flopping down in my recliner. "Maybe if this stupid publicity stunt of yours ever starts to work, I'll get the chance."

"Keep—you should excuse the expression—your shirt on, dolling. I'm working on something now, something special."

My heart skipped a beat, and I sat forward excitedly.

"What?" I demanded. "What is it?"

"It's too soon to talk about it, Chickie, but, trust me when I tell you, it's big, you're gonna love it!"

"Morty, *tell* me!"

"Nah, seriously, I don't want to get your hopes up until I know a little more. Meanwhile, how'd it go today?"

I told him all about Larchmont and the Other Brandies and my unorthodox solution.

"Denk goodness you figured it out, dolling. You don't finish the commercial, I'm not sure you get paid. Speaking of which, about your advance…."

"Did you talk to Mr. and Mrs. Akers?"

"Unfortunately, they're out of town, but—"

"Argh," I grouched.

"—but don't worry, they'll be beck in the office tomorrow efternoon, I got an appointment. And even if they won't spring for an advance, Chickie, I'll stop by on Thursday and front you some more cash, so you can pay your rent on Friday. That's okay with you?"

"Yeah, great, Morty, thanks!"

Though I hadn't gotten much sleep the night before and I was wasted from my long day at the studio, I lay awake till after midnight, turning over the events of the last few days in my head.

Dr. Le Groth's radio, Fido's bowl, Phil's watch, Moonchild's vest, Libby's hair dryer, Jeff's razor….

I tried counting sheep, but they kept morphing into little lamb chops as they frolicked around my mental meadow, so I pushed them out of the way and counted questions, instead.

Had Phil's watch really been stolen, or not?

Why had Phil visited Dr. Le Groth's room in the dead of night?

Why couldn't I find Dr. Le Groth anywhere on the internet, and what had he been hiding under his pillow?

Why had Moonchild been eavesdropping outside Miss Robert's door?

What was Miss Roberts' first name?

Why hadn't anything been stolen from her, or from *me*?

How come Libby and Jeff were always biting each other's heads off?

Was Libby a kleptomaniac?

Was someone else?

Was the thief a resident or someone from the outside?

What was the motive behind the Roomy Toilet thefts?

Who was the thief?

Who?

What?

How?

And why?

Why?

Why?

I never did hear Libby and Phil come in. From my nest way up at the top of the house, I'm not sure I *would* have heard them. All I know is that I didn't.

As I finally drifted off to Z-land, one more troubling question floated across my mind. Earlier, when I'd found Libby's door standing open, I'd assumed that she'd accidentally left it that way when she and Phil went out for the evening.

Was it Libby who'd left her door open, though—or had someone else been inside her room?

June's Log: June 6

My heart just wasn't in my yoga, and, for the first time I can remember, I finished my routine feeling less centered and more stressed out than I was when I started.

Downstairs, things weren't any better. There was an awful lot of "please" and "thank you" at breakfast, but very little conversation. Dr. Le Groth never said a single word to anyone, Miss Roberts wasn't even there, and Moonchild, who usually lingered over coffee, mumbled something about grabbing a smoke and left the table early, slamming the front door behind him. Phil made a few desultory notes in his little pad, but soon gave up and put it away.

Since it was a weekday, Jeff was in a suit and tie, but of course he hadn't shaved.

"You're not going into the office like that, are you?" Libby said, and the edge to her voice rivaled the X-ACTO knives I'd seen on Jeff's work table.

"I guess I'll *have* to," he snapped, "since *somebody* walked off with my razor."

"Don't start that again," said Phil. "Listen, you can borrow mine, if you want. You can *have* mine."

"Not interested. I notice *you* haven't lost anything to our sticky-fingered friend—at least, if that story about your watch was true, and you weren't just covering up for—"

"*I* haven't lost anything, either," I said. I didn't like calling attention to that fact, but it seemed more important to defuse the tension between Jeff and Phil before they started throwing things at each other.

"Neither has Miss Roberts," Libby added. "So what does *that* prove?"

Things were getting *really* uncomfortable at the Roomy Toilet, and I knew we needed to get our hands on a bottle of Ti-D-Bowl soon, before the whole boarding house went down the drain.

"Everybody's mad at everybody else," I said to Mrs. Smedleigh, as I helped her clear away the breakfast dishes. "We have to *do* something."

"Well, of course we do, dear, but *what*?" She rinsed the plates and cups in the sink and handed them to me to stack in the dishwasher. "I'm thinking of simply asking everyone to *leave* and shutting this place down for a while, then starting over again in a month or two."

I was stunned. "You *can't*! This is our *home!*"

She sighed. "That's a lovely sentiment, June. But you and Philip have only just arrived, and Miss Roberts and Moonchild and Mr. Le Groth haven't—"

"Dr. Le Groth."

"—*Dr.* Le Groth haven't been here much longer. Jeff and Libby have been with me for several years, though, and I suppose this *is* their home by now." She turned the last juice glass over and over beneath the stream of hot water. "It just doesn't *feel* like home anymore, not with all these horrid things happening, not with all of you so *angry*."

"I wish there was something I could do to help."

She handed me the glass. "You *are* helping, dear. You're a—"

"No, I mean *really* help," I said, sliding the top tray into the dishwasher and closing the door.

She dried her hands on a dish towel and passed it over. "Well, then, would you mind checking on Miss Roberts for me? Make sure she's all right?"

"Sure thing!"

I ran up to the second floor and tapped on the spinster's door. There was no response. I banged loudly enough to wake her, but still nothing.

She wasn't in there.

When the echoes of my pounding died away, I realized how very quiet the house was. Phil, Libby, Jeff, and Dr. Le Groth had all gone off to work, Mrs. Smedleigh was down in the kitchen, and, if Moonchild had come back in from the porch, he was apparently squirreled away upstairs in his room.

I touched a hand to Miss Roberts' door.

Investigating, I thought, wasn't getting me anywhere worth going.

If Mrs. S kicked us all out of the Roomy Toilet, I could always just say forget about Morty's dumb emancipation stunt—which hadn't yet garnered me a single column inch of publicity, anyway—and go home to Mom and Pops, but what about the rest of them? Where would *they* go?

No, I *had* to find out who was stealing from our rooms and put a stop to the thefts before it was too late.

Almost as if they had a mind of their own, my fingertips delicately traced the line of the wood grain down to the doorknob.

I'd been inside every room in the house, I realized, except this one.

The brass knob was cool to my touch.

Sometimes, I thought, you reach a point where you *have* to snoop.

I took a deep breath and tightened my fingers.

And, in a house where no one ever locked their doors, the knob wouldn't turn.

For Allie and Brenna, it was the first full day of summer vacation, and we'd arranged to meet at the Half Moon Café, our favorite coffee shop, at two. I left the house a little early, iPhone in my pocket and earbuds in my ears, in order to have time to make a quick stop at the Mercantile

Bank. I still had about eighty dollars of the hundred Morty'd given me, and I wanted to deposit it into my account; with things disappearing from the Roomy Toilet left and right, I didn't feel comfortable leaving cash lying around in my room, and I certainly didn't want to be carrying that much money around with me.

As I left the bank—with one twenty-dollar bill still in my pocket for mad money—Miss Roberts was just coming in. Despite the warmth of the day, she wore a long skirt and a long-sleeved blouse, and she had a sweater draped around her shoulders and a black leather pocketbook clutched tightly in both hands.

"June," she said tightly. "I hope you are *saving* your money for your education and not withdrawing it frivolously."

"Yes, ma'am," I said. "I just made a deposit."

"Very good. I am about to do the same." She pursed her lips, then made an expression which I suppose was intended to be a smile. "If you would care to wait a few moments, I can offer you a ride back to the house."

"Oh, no, thank you, ma'am. I'm meeting some of my friends in a minute."

"How nice. Have a pleasant day." And she walked on past me without waiting for a response.

When the light changed, I started across the street—and jerked to a stop halfway at the sight of Moonchild sitting on the sidewalk, right next to the Half Moon's door, in faded camouflage fatigues, his wild hair almost hidden beneath a red bandana. His Super Bowl cap lay upside down between his outstretched legs, and, as I stood frozen in the middle of the street, a businessman threw some loose change into the hat, hardly breaking his stride.

Again, like yesterday morning on the porch, I didn't know whether to be fascinated or horrified. I've seen street people begging before— sometimes, depending on my mood and the state of my finances, I'll contribute the odd quarter, and once I stopped to listen to a young Oriental woman play an achingly beautiful piece on the violin and put a dollar in her case before walking on. But this was someone I *knew*, and watching him solicit passersby for a donation made me *really* uncomfortable.

Truth be told, it wasn't so much that *I* was uncomfortable—although there was some of that going on inside me, too. Mainly, though, I didn't want to embarrass Moonchild. If he turned out to be the Roomy Toilet's thief, after all, I didn't care *how* he felt, but I kind of liked the poor old hippie. I didn't want him to be Mr. Rip-Off, and I didn't want to make him feel worse about himself than he probably already did.

So, what to do? Should I breeze right past him and pretend I didn't see him? Should I stop and talk with him but not give him any money? I *couldn't* help him out, even if I wanted to: all I had left after making my deposit was that twenty-dollar bill, and I wasn't giving him *that*! Maybe the best thing would be to call Brenna's cell phone—Allie's parents still live in the Twentieth Century, so they won't let her have one—and have the girls meet me somewhere else.

Fortunately, the problem was solved when Moonchild got to his feet, emptied the accumulated change out of his ballcap, scrunched the cap down on top of his bandana and shambled off in the direction of the pay phone down the block.

Relieved, I dashed the rest of the way across the street before the light changed and went into the Half Moon, the dark, rich aroma of freshly roasted coffee almost overwhelming me as I came through the door.

Allie and Brenna were already there, sitting at our favorite table in the back, and Edie, the owner, was taking orders at the register. I waved at A and B and told Edie I'd have a caramel frappuccino.

"You want it skinny, right, hon?" she asked, as she took my twenty and made change.

"I want it absolutely *emaciated*," I said, and dropped a quarter into the tip jar.

Edie made my drink, and I carried it back to join my friends.

When the three of us were eight, we invented a complicated secret handshake that took about a minute to work through and made us look like a team of contortionists. By the time we hit the ripe old age of ten, though, it had gotten much too embarrassing to perform in public, and by eleven, it just seemed sort of stupid. All that was left of it now was the second it took to lay our right hands on the table and touch our fingertips together. On each of our right wrists were two friendship bracelets woven out of multicolored embroidery thread. Each of us had made one for each of the others. They lasted about six months to a year, and, whenever one wore out and fell away, the girl who'd made it would replace it with a new one.

For the instant our hands connected on the tabletop, we looked like a scene out of Disney's "It's a Small World" ride. Allie, who's been my very best friend since I was in kindergarten, is black and beautiful, with the bearing of an African princess. Her parents, unfortunately, are divorced. Her father served a term as mayor—and then, when he was up for re-election, her mother ran against him ... and won! Brenna is Korean-American—both her parents were born in Seoul and emigrated to the US in the Seventies—with gorgeous amber skin and long glossy jet-black straight hair. Her dad teaches art history at the community college, and her mom's my dentist.

"I heart summer vacation!" Brenna sang.

"Three whole months without homework," Allie agreed.

We sat there, sipping our drinks and chattering away. They told me who'd gotten in trouble during the last week of school, who was heading off to summer camp, who was crushing on whom these days. I filled them in on my emancipation and move to the Roomy Toilet—I felt really bad not admitting the whole thing was a gimmick, but I'd promised Morty I wouldn't, so I didn't—and introduced the cast of characters.

"You know how we used to remember the names of Snow White's Seven Dwarves?"

"Two S's, two D's, three Emotions," Brenna said promptly.

"Sleepy Sneezy, Dopey Doc, and Cheerful Bashful Grumpy," Allie chanted.

"Well, it's kind of like that at the boarding house: three Oldies, three twenty-somethings, and one Combo Plate. The Oldies are Mrs. Smedleigh, Dr. Le Groth, and Miss Roberts. Mrs. S is the landlady—she's really sweet, but she totally needs a makeover. Dr. Le Groth and Miss Roberts are both kind of crabby, although he's nicer than she is. Libby and Phil and Jeff are all in their twenties—Libby and Jeff work together, but they're always at each other's throats. I think she and Phil are getting to be an item—they went out to a movie last night, and they must have come back pretty late. And the Combo Plate is Moonchild. He—"

"Moonchild? Is that his name?"

"Well, not really, but it's what he likes to be called. He's like this leftover hippie. He calls everybody 'man.' He doesn't have a job—something happened to him in the Army, and he's kind of like not all there anymore slash he doesn't *wash*."

"What *does* he do?"

I thought about telling them I'd just seen him outside the Half Moon, begging, but decided to leave that part out. "He just sort of hangs out," I said.

And then I told them about the thefts, and of course they wanted to know whodunit.

"I've been trying to figure that out. I don't see why Mrs. Smedleigh would be stealing from her own tenants, that just doesn't make any sense. Libby's much too nice to be doing it. Phil's nice, too, but something's definitely going on with him: he had this really expensive watch that got swiped, but the second I suggested calling the police, he suddenly 'remembered' it wasn't stolen, after all. It was in the shop."

"He's afraid of the cops," said Brenna, who would skip her own graduation before she'd miss a rerun of *Law & Order*.

"Exactly. And the same day Dr. Le Groth's radio disappeared—the day after Phil moved in—the two of them had this late-night confab in the doctor's room, which neither one of them has ever said a word about since. And Phil's always writing stuff down in this little notebook, and Dr. Le Groth's been away a lot and doesn't show up anywhere on the internet. It makes me think they both must be up to something, or two different somethings, but I can't figure out what."

"What about Jeff?"

"I haven't decided about him. He seems like a decent guy, but he and Libby totally bring out the worst in each other. I could sort of imagine him taking her hair dryer, just to torch her off—or her taking his razor—but why would either one of them steal Dr. Le Groth's radio, or Moonchild's vest, or Fido's *bowl*? That's what I keep coming back to: why?"

"What about Moonchild? Could he be doing it?"

"He's such a stoner, I guess anything's possible—but, again, *why*? The other night I saw him listening at Miss Roberts' door, which was weird. I mean, what was *that* all about? She's the only one who hasn't been robbed, yet, so maybe that says she's the one who's been—"

"Are you saying *you've* been robbed, too, June?" Allie breathed.

"Oh, no, well, her and me."

"So maybe that says *you* did it," Brenna said. "Did you ever think of that?"

"Hey, that reminds me," Allie said, rummaging in her backpack and handing over a paperback book with a red cover. "I just finished this last night, June. You have *got* to read it. It's *old*—it came out before we were born, like around 2000 or something—but it's hella cool."

The title printed on the cover read *the curious incident of the dog in the night-time*, all in lower-case letters, and underneath that was the cutout shape of an upside-down dog with a puffball tail—sort of like Larchmont.

"It's about this fifteen-year-old boy in England," Allie said eagerly, "who has, like, autism or something, only he solves this mystery about a dead dog in his neighborhood."

"Maybe it'll help me figure out *our* mystery," I said hopefully.

Allie's eyes glistened. "That would be so awesome!"

"How come June gets to read it first?" Brenna complained, cueing Allie into one of the Abbott and Costello routines they've been perfecting ever since a long-ago sleepover when we watched *Valley Girl* maybe one time too many.

"Oh, like you read books," Allie said.

"I read books, you jerk!"

"Brenna, the last book you read was *The Baby-Sitter's Club*."

"What's wrong with *The Baby-Sitter's Club*?"

"Nothing—if you're a baby."

"Well, *you*'re still a member of the Pen 15 Club."

"Oh, my God, that is *so* mature."

Brenna's cell phone chirped. She dumped the contents of her beaded hobo bag onto the table and found it in the litter of loose coins, lipsticks, hair brush, extra scrunchies, tissues, lip balm. She checked the screen and rolled her eyes. "It's just my boyfriend," she said. "I'll call him later. This is girl time."

"You have a boyfriend?" I said. "When did *this* happen?"

"It's *Jaaaaay*-son," Allie said, stretching the name out for several seconds. "He's a boy, and he's *maybe* her friend, but he is not her *boy*friend."

"He totally *is*."

"You *wish*."

"I *know*."

"You wouldn't know what to do with a boyfriend if you *did* have one."

"I know *exactly* what to do with a boyfriend, duh."

"Oh, yeah? What?"

"We—" Brenna blushed and fell out of character. "I am so not talking about this with you."

"Don't be ridiculous," Allie said. "Of course you are. Let's—"

"What are you two doing after this?" I said, cutting Brenna a break and changing the subject.

Allie seemed reluctant to let it drop, but I dug an elbow into her side, and she clucked her tongue and huffed out a sigh. "It's such a beautiful day," she said, "I'm going for a walk in the park."

"Did you bring your iPhone?" I asked.

"She doesn't *have* an iPhone," Brenna teased.

"I don't *need* an iPhone, Brenna. The birds are my iPhone."

My friends are nuts, but I love them!

As I left the Half Moon, half an hour later, a striking woman with skin the color of mocha approached me. She wore a knee-length blue dress and carried an oversized fabric handbag slung over her left shoulder.

"Julie Jefferson," she said crisply. "With the *Straight Shooter*. I wonder if you'd be willing to answer a few questions?"

Finally, I thought, *some publicity! Excellent!*

"Sure," I said, shaking the hand she offered. "Shoot!"

She smiled politely. "Do you mind if I record?"

Without waiting for an answer, she took a miniature digital recorder from her bag and flicked it on. "Testing," she said. "Testing, one, two, three." She played it back—the sound quality was great for such a little thing!—then rewound to the beginning of the tape and held the recorder up between us.

"For starters," she said, "can you say your name and then slowly spell it for me, please?"

That was odd. Shouldn't she already *have* my name?

"Is this about the emancipation?" I asked.

"Say what?"

"My emancipation? From my parents? Isn't that what you want to talk about?"

She switched off the recorder. "No, honey," she said. "I'm just getting some reaction quotes for a sidebar on the crime wave."

"A what on the what?"

"A sidebar—a little human-interest story they'll run next to the main news story—about the latest bank robbery?"

The penny dropped.

"So this isn't about my court case? About my career?"

She looked at me blankly. "Your career?"

I shook my head in disgust and walked away. I was going to *murder* Morty the next time I saw him.

My iPhone battery ran down halfway back to the Roomy Toilet, so I let the birds, the dogs, and the traffic provide the soundtrack as I trudged the rest of the way across town, my backpack feeling heavier with every step.

When I finally turned onto Smedley Street, Dylan and Carson were coming towards me, tossing an earth-caked garden trowel back and forth between them.

"What are you two up to?" I greeted them.

"Nothing," Dylan said quickly, stuffing the blade of the trowel into the back pocket of what seemed to be the same jeans he'd been wearing on Saturday.

"Still got my autograph, Carson?"

The littler boy stuck out his arm proudly. It was five days since I'd signed him, but my message and name were still clearly visible on his skin. He apparently hadn't changed *his* clothes all week, either. Or bathed.

"Too bad you can't play with Mrs. Smedleigh's sign anymore, huh?"

"Least we don't have to keep carrying that stupid ladder around," said Dylan.

"It's not a ladder," Carson reminded him.

"That stupid *step*ladder."

"Where do kids your age come up with these ideas, anyway?"

"Dylan is creep-o-shuss," Carson said.

"The word is 'precocious,' Snot Brain," said Dylan.

"The word for *you* is creep-o-shuss," said Carson, "and I'm not a snotbrain."

"You're a creep-o-shuss Snot Brain."

"Well, *you're* a creep-o-shuss Fart Head."

"You're *both* pretty creep-o-shuss, messing around with other people's property," I said.

"Mind your own beeswax, lady," Dylan said. "You're not the boss of me!"

"Me, neither," Carson agreed.

"Speaking of which," I said, "where'd you get that trowel?"

"What trowel?" Dylan said.

"The one in your back pocket?"

"That's not a towel," Carson said.

"I know," I said, "it's a *step*towel."

"It's a little shovel," Carson said.

"It's a trowel," I said. "Where did you get it?"

"We found it," Dylan said—at the exact same moment Carson said, "She wasn't using it."

"Who wasn't using it?"

"That other lady, back there." Carson pointed in the direction of the Roomy Toilet.

"That's stealing," I said.

"She wasn't *using* it," Carson insisted.

"So if you're not riding your bicycle," I said, "I'm allowed to take it?"

"I don't *have* a bicycle," the boy complained, "just a stupid tricycle."

"And when you're not riding it," I persisted, "I'm allowed to take it?"

"No!" Carson wailed. "It's *mine!*"

"Ah," I said and held out my hand.

Dylan grudgingly pulled the trowel from his pocket and passed it over. "Who wants your stupid autograph, anyway?" he said. "It's probably full of cooties." He spit on Carson's arm and rubbed at my signature with his grimy fist.

"Don't you spit on me!" Carson yelled and spat right into his stepbrother's face.

"You are *so* dead," Dylan yelled back and spat at Carson, who ducked out of the way—

—so Dylan's germy gob of saliva landed right on the front of my shirt.

"*Gross!*" I cried, totally disgusted, and took off at a run for the house.

Mrs. Smedleigh was on her hands and knees in the little patch of garden to the left of the porch steps, pulling tiny weeds from between the azalea bush and the rhododendron. She somehow managed to look elegant, even in well-worn old overalls and green gloves, a straw sunhat protecting her beehive.

"Hi, Mrs. S," I panted, stopping to catch my breath and pass over the trowel. "Is this yours?"

"Why, yes, dear, I was just looking for it. Wherever did you find it?"

"Those same two boys who changed your sign," I said. "Look what they did to my shirt!"

She pulled off a glove and rubbed the wet spot between her thumb and forefinger. "Is this—?"

"Little-boy spit," I said. "It's not going to stain, is it?"

"No, no, dear. It's just water, really, with a *soupçon* of snips and snails and puppy-dog tails."

"Soup's on?"

"*Soupçon*, dear. It means 'a little bit.' It's French. Now you run upstairs and change, and then bring your blouse back down to me, and I'll wash this right out for you."

"I don't want to be any trouble."

"It's no trouble at all, dear. Go, go, go!"

The bathroom door on the second landing was open, and Libby was on her hands and knees, scrubbing the tiled floor.

"Is Mrs. S on strike?" I said, pausing in the doorway to watch.

Libby looked up. She wasn't wearing any makeup, and for the first time, I noticed that she had a spray of light freckles across her cheekbones. "No," she sighed, pushing her hair off one eye with a rubber-gloved hand. "I spilled a bottle of body lotion, and I just didn't think it was fair to make her clean up after my carelessness. Meanwhile"—she looked up at the wet spot on my shirt, her big hazel eyes sparkling in the overhead light—"what happened to *you*?"

I told her about Dylan and Carson and their little spitfest.

"Boys," she commiserated.

"They *will* be boys," I said, using my most adult voice.

"And you know the worst thing, June?"

"No, what?"

"Sooner or later," she said, "they turn into *men*."

In the silence that followed that remark, I wondered if she was talking about men in general, or one individual man in particular.

"Hey, that's nice," I said, sniffing the air and changing the subject. The aroma was sweet, a little fruity, very distinctive. "What is it?"

"Cucumber melon," she said. "It was practically a new bottle, and I just flushed most of it down the toilet."

"Is there any left?"

"In the sink," she said. "Help yourself."

The bottle was, in fact, practically empty, but I squirted a dab of the pale-green cream onto my palm, washed my hands together, cupped them around my nose, and took a deep whiff. "I *like* this," I said.

"Take the bottle. I think I'm pretty much *done* with it, at this point."

"Thanks, Libby!" I tucked it into my backpack and skipped on up the remaining two flights of stairs to my room to change.

It wasn't until I'd brought my spat-upon shirt back down to Mrs. Smedley and she'd tossed it into the washing machine in the laundry room off the kitchen that it hit me.

Yesterday, I'd considered the possibility that the Roomy Toilet's thief was an outsider. And today, I'd actually *caught* neighborhood terrors Dylan and Carson stealing Mrs. Smedley's trowel.

Had I stumbled accidentally across the solution to the crimes?

After all, the sliding glass door in the kitchen was almost always open. If the boys were ripping stuff off from the garden, why couldn't they be ripping stuff off from inside the house, too?

No, I thought, *that's nuts, Dr. Le Groth's radio was taken in the middle of the night, when Dylan and Carson were home in bed, sound asleep.*

Or were they? How the heck would I know?

But I locked the kitchen door last night. They couldn't have gotten in to take Jeff's razor.

No, wait, the razor was already gone *by then—and there hasn't been another theft since....*

I pounded the heel of my right hand against my forehead, trying to knock out the idea of two larcenous masterminds whose combined ages barely equaled my fourteen years. I mean, swiping a trowel from the garden was one thing, but coming into the house and stealing from people's rooms? Over and over again, risking discovery every time?

No way! Dylan and Carson were creep-o-shuss little monsters, sure, but they weren't *criminals*—or *idiots*, for that matter.

Were they?

Before dinner, I was sitting out on the porch swing, reading *the curious incident of the dog in the night-time*. Cars went by on Smedley Street, a squirrel scampered across the yard, and a pair of power walkers waved at me as they whizzed past the house.

The book was really interesting, but as I read teenage narrator Christopher John Francis Boone's explanation of why Marilyn vos Savant, the World's Smartest Woman, was right about the Monty Hall Problem, a neighborhood dog started barking in the distance, and I found my mind beginning to drift.

A barking dog, *the curious incident of the dog in the night-time*, Downward Facing Dog, Upward Facing Dog, Greedily Gobbling Dog, Larchmont the Bichon Frise, Danny and Manny, the Other Brandies, Yummy Nibbles, Mikey not-stealing Thin Mints and Do-Si-Dos, the missing Oreos, a ten-pound bag of cat food, Fido's bowl....

Oh, no.

At that moment, a number of things I'd noticed over the course of the week suddenly fell into their proper arrangement, and I realized who'd been responsible for at least *one* of the thefts from the Roomy Toilet, and why.

Oh, *no*!

I didn't think this one was connected to any of the others—I *hoped* it wasn't—but the puzzle pieces fit together perfectly, and I knew I was right.

The knowledge was scary, all by itself, but the scariest part was that I had absolutely no idea what to do about it.

Dinner that night was awkward. Everyone acted suspicious of everyone else, Dr. Le Groth was more cantankerous and Miss Roberts crabbier than usual, Libby and Jeff hardly spoke to each other, and the usually placid Moonchild and Phil Marlowe barely managed to be civil. Even Fido turned up a haughty nose at the stuffed mouse on a string with which I tried to tempt him.

Meanwhile, for the first time since I'd arrived on Smedley Street, the meal Mrs. Smedleigh dished up for us was hard to swallow. The pork chops were overcooked, the mashed potatoes were lumpy, and the string beans were, well, sort of stringy. Mrs. S was obviously distracted by the tension in the house, and her cooking was paying the price.

After an uncomfortable half hour at the table, Dr. Le Groth went into the parlor to watch the news on TV, and I brought my laptop downstairs to check my email. There was no progress in the Middle East peace talks, no new leads on the local bank robberies, and nothing in my inbox but spam, spam, and more spam.

I was in bed reading by eight-thirty, and even Melvin Spellbound and his Uncle Borgel couldn't put a smile on my face. I gave up before Borgel finished explaining why time is like a map of New Jersey, switched off my lamp, and went to sleep.

It must have been about eleven when the scream woke me up.

At first, I thought I must have dreamt it. But then I heard the clatter of feet on the stairs and the clamor of confused voices from somewhere below, and I realized I was awake and something had happened.

I put on my slippers and ran downstairs in my pjs to find Mrs. Smedleigh and the rest of the boarders gathered around a completely distressed Miss Roberts in the parlor. They were all in their night clothes: Jeff in a ratty old bathrobe, Phil in gray sweats, Libby in a pink nightie, Dr. Le Groth in striped pajama pants and a satin smoking jacket, Moonchild in cut-off denim shorts and an old bowling shirt with the name "Angelo" stitched over the breast pocket in blue script letters.

"It's gone!" cried Miss Roberts, holding the neck of her flowered housecoat tight at her throat. "*Gone!*"

"What's gone, madam?" Dr. Le Groth demanded.

"My satchel! It was in my closet. I went to—to put something into it, and it was gone! Which of you horrible people took it? I want that satchel returned, and I want it returned *immediately!*"

"What's it look like, man?"

"It's a brown leather bag, a Gladstone bag, about *this* big"—she held her hands about two feet apart, then moved them to indicate width and height—"with handles and straps and brass fastenings. It's a *satchel*, it looks like a leather bag!"

"It's okay, Miss Roberts," Phil said. "Calm down. We'll find it."

"What was in it?" asked Libby.

"My—my Bible," the spinster said, flustered. "My family Bible, we've had it for generations!"

No wonder she was so upset.

"I've had enough of this nonsense," Mrs. Smedleigh announced with fierce determination. "We can't go on pretending nothing is happening here. I am telephoning the police."

"No!" Miss Roberts shrieked. "No police! I—"

She choked off whatever she'd been about to say and took several deep breaths. "I want to give the thief a chance to repent and return it—to return all the stolen items. That—I know that's the Christian thing to do."

I sidled closer to Moonchild and tugged at his sleeve, and he bent down until his shaggy head was right next to my face. "I saw you listening at her door Sunday night," I whispered. "If you took her bag, you *have* to give it back."

We turned our heads so he could whisper into *my* ear, and I could smell the tobacco on his breath. "*I* saw *you* trying to get into her room this morning," he said softly. "Did *you* take it, man?"

I stared at him. How had he seen me? He'd been out on the porch at the time—hadn't he?

Before I could think how to respond, he spoke again. "I won't tell if you don't, man. Deal?"

Terrific: either I entered into a conspiracy of silence with a burnout who might just *turn* out to be the Roomy Toilet Marauder, after all, or I'd have to explain to Miss Roberts and the rest of them what I was doing trying to bust into her bedroom on the same day it was burglarized.

I made my decision.

"Deal," I said.

I looked up to see Dr. Le Groth stroking his bushy mustache soberly. "We're all agreed, then," he said—and, for one panicky moment, I thought he was talking about the arrangement I'd just made with Moonchild. "We will give the thief until suppertime tomorrow to return all of the stolen items to their owners. If full restitution has not been made by that time, then we will delay no further and call in the local police."

"*Les gendarmes*," Mrs. Smedleigh said tightly. "That's French."

June's Log: June 7

I bolted upright from a nightmare in which I was being chased down an endless corridor by a huge buzzing razor in a fringed leather vest and reached for the comforting softness of my friend Bennington.

He wasn't there.

I looked under my top sheet and blanket—but he wasn't there, either.

My bear was gone!

Someone had come into my room at night while I slept and stolen my bear!

I wanted to scream more loudly than Miss Roberts had screamed last night. I wanted to start punching people in the head and keep punching them until they gave Bennie back to me. I wanted to cry.

Don't panic, I told myself. *Keep it together, June.*

I sat up in bed and forced myself to think through the situation again.

A radio, a cat's bowl, a leather vest, a hair dryer, a razor, a satchel, a family Bible.

A teddy bear?

All little things, inexpensive, impersonal.

Except *this* was personal, all right! There's no way you can take my bear and get away with it, you rotten—

Calm down, girl. Calm down and think!

Maybe the thief *wanted* us all upset. Maybe that was the point of the thefts, just to get on our nerves and set us against each other.

So, what if I reacted differently than everyone else had, just sat on Bennington's disappearance for a while and didn't let on that he was missing?

If I didn't acknowledge that I, too, had been robbed, maybe that might flush the thief out into the open.

And if it didn't have that effect, I could always start screaming and punching and crying later on.

For now, though, I got out of bed very deliberately, put on my leotard, and started stretching.…

Jeff, Miss Roberts, and Dr. Le Groth were already at the table when I walked into the dining room, and not one of them seemed surprised that I wasn't all weepy and proclaiming myself the Roomy Toilet's latest victim—which meant, I figured, either something or nothing.

Mrs. Smedleigh hadn't even cooked today: instead, six boxes of cereal were lined up in the center of the table, along with a platter of bananas, strawberries, and peaches.

I sliced a banana into my bowl and covered it with Raisin Bran and milk.

"Hi, Moonchild," I said, as the aging hippie appeared from the stairs in a faded denim work shirt and shotgunned jeans.

"Hey, man," he said glumly, taking his seat and reaching for the Count Chocula.

A minute later, Jeff looked up as Libby and Phil arrived together.

"Late night?" he said.

Libby regarded him with disdain. "What's that supposed to mean?"

"Your eyes are bloodshot," Jeff pointed out. "Doesn't look like you got much sleep." He arched his eyebrows suggestively and tilted his head towards Phil. "Hot date?"

"You're disgusting," Libby said. "And for your information—not that it's any of your business—I think I'm coming down with a cold."

Her eyes *were* a little red, I noticed, but she didn't sound sick.

What *was* going on between her and Phil?

"Did you run this morning?" I asked, trying to steer the conversation into calmer waters.

"Of course," she said, annoyed even with me. "I run *every* morning, you know that."

Miss Roberts threw down her spoon. "I've had all of this—this inane *small talk* I can take. You all seem to forget I have been *robbed* of my most precious possession. I am leaving this house, Mrs. Smedleigh."

"Hey, come on, man," said Moonchild. "We agreed to give the thief like twenty-four hours to turn himself in."

"Or herself," Jeff interjected, glaring angrily at Libby Justice.

"Whatever, man."

"You don't want to break your promise, Miss Roberts, do you?" I said. "That'd be a shame."

"Practically a *sin*," Phil suggested.

Miss Roberts took in a deep breath and sniffed it out again. "Very well, then," she decided, "I shall wait until six o'clock this evening, but then I am leaving. I won't spend another night under this roof."

Once those who went to work had left the house, I spent the next few hours in the parlor, going over it and over it in my mind, again and again, trying desperately to wrestle all of my questions and the few scanty facts I had in my possession into an order that made something resembling sense.

I knew *I* wasn't in any danger from the police, because I knew I hadn't stolen anything. Even if Moonchild went back on the deal we'd made and ratted me out, I hadn't done anything *wrong*. Sure, I'd had my hand on Miss Roberts' doorknob, had even tried to turn it. But it was locked, and in actual fact I'd neither entered her room nor even been able to open her door.

No, I hadn't taken Miss Roberts' satchel—but *someone* had, and I knew what was bound to happen if I wasn't able to pinpoint the guilty party.

Because there was that *other* theft I was sure about, that *other* thief I was in a position to name—and that one was someone I wanted to protect, not expose.

Once the cops were on the scene, though, there was every chance they'd figure out the truth, and the one person I wanted to keep out of hot water would probably wind up drowning in it.

With every minute that passed, we were one minute closer to the point of no return, the point when the police would be called, the point when it would be too late to keep the situation under control.

Mrs. Smedleigh came in with Fido at her heels and ran a duster over the lamps, the coffee table, and the bookshelves. Miss Roberts, who never even glanced at the TV when Dr. Le Groth was watching the news, turned it on and stared at a soap for five minutes, then snapped it off with a cluck of her tongue and stormed up to her room. Moonchild spent most of the day on the front porch, smoking. I didn't hear a word out of any of them, not one single syllable.

If only the person responsible for all those other thefts would admit it—or even just stash the stolen items in some out-of-the-way corner and make an anonymous phone call saying, "Hey, go check under the dining room table," or wherever.

But time passed, and there was no ringing phone, no happy cry of discovery from another room. And it was one o'clock and two o'clock, and Libby and Phil and Jeff and Dr. Le Groth would all be home by five-thirty—and then it would be six o'clock and too darned late.

The seven of us sat in the parlor, waiting for Mrs. Smedleigh.

We'd gathered in the dining room at six, as usual, but there were no plates on the table, no silverware, no glasses, no napkins—and no smells of cooking wafted out from the kitchen. As if by some unspoken signal, we all trooped into the parlor to await whatever was going to happen next.

I sat on the end of the sofa closest to the dining room and fiddled nervously with the Boggle cubes, which were still in their plastic tray on the coffee table. Libby settled on the sofa's other end, and Jeff, Moonchild, Miss Roberts, Phil, and Dr. Le Groth turned the five armchairs and ranged them in a semicircle around the coffee table and sat. Beneath the table, Fido lay curled up in a ball, eyes closed, his little chest rising and falling regularly. At least *someone* was relaxed.

None of the rest of us seemed to have any idea what to do or say. We just sat there and waited, motionless, meek, mute.

Finally, the sound of footsteps approached from the back of the house.

The garish colors Mrs. Smedleigh normally draped herself in were gone. As if she were in mourning, she had changed into a black cardigan and slacks. She'd even toned down her makeup and brushed her hair out of its beehive. Oddly, she wound up looking *younger* than usual, but the liveliness that normally danced in her eyes was gone.

She squeezed past me and sat heavily between me and Libby on the couch.

"Well," she said, and her voice was flat and tired. "It's time. Before I place the call, does anyone have anything to say?"

We looked at each other uneasily.

Dr. Le Groth cleared his throat.

"I," Jeff began, but then he shook his head and lapsed back into silence.

Libby looked like she was about to cry.

And suddenly I realized that we were arranged like the cast of characters in the final scene of a TV murder mystery, waiting for the Great Detective to guide us through the solution to the week's dastardly crime.

All we were missing was a Great Detective.

If I was ever going to make it as an actress, I decided, this was my moment. Maybe, if I plunged right in and acted like I knew what I was talking about, the thief would slip up and make the mistake I'd been hoping for all day.

My mind raced with possibilities. The easiest thing would be to throw the blame onto Dylan and Carson. I was convinced they hadn't done anything worse than graffiti the ROOM TO LET sign a few times and swipe Mrs. Smedleigh's garden trowel, but at least casting a couple of aspersions in their direction might buy me enough time to dream up something better.

I couldn't bring myself to do it, though. Dylan and Carson might well be a pair of creep-o-shuss little neighborhood brats, but they were *kids*, and I couldn't go dragging their names through the mud, not even for a good cause.

But I had to do *something*. I couldn't just sit here and watch the Roomy Toilet get flushed.

Oh, well, I thought. *Here goes nothing....*

I turned abruptly to my left and faced our landlady.

"I do," I said. "Let's start with the theft that makes the least amount of sense. Who stole Fido's dish from Mrs. Smedleigh's kitchen?"

Her brow furrowed. "I—"

"You don't know," I said. "But maybe we can figure it out by the process of elimination. The first person I suspected was"—I whirled pretty much at random and pointed an accusatory finger— "Moonchild!"

He leaned away from me as if I'd poked him with a ten-foot Albanian and stuck up his hands in horror. "No, man," he cried, "I totally didn't take it, I swear!"

That seemed pretty convincing—unless he, too, was acting. "Yes, my reasoning convinced me of your innocence," I said, making it up as I went along. "Well, then, I thought, if it wasn't Moonchild, was it—?"

And at that point, Mrs. Smedleigh suddenly interrupted me. "Stop, dear, please." She peered beneath the coffee table to make sure Fido was still asleep. "I know you're trying to help," she said, pitching her voice so low it was hard to hear her, "but the truth is that Fido's bowl wasn't stolen at all."

I did a double take. "It wasn't?"

"No, dear, no one *stole* it. I just threw it away. I've always hated that old thing."

"But—then why did you say it was stolen?"

"It was Dr. Le Groth's radio going missing that gave me the idea. Fido loved that silly bowl so much, he'd never have forgiven me for junking it. If it was stolen, though, well, he'd just *have* to get used to a new one! So I, well, I made the whole thing up!"

You see? The moment I started stirring the pot, the truth began to float to the surface! Sweet!

Now if only the rest of it would come that easily!

I gathered my thoughts and plunged on. "The most confusing thing about these thefts was the question of motive. Why would someone go to all the trouble and risk of stealing inexpensive items, when most of them could have been purchased for a couple of dollars at any department store? Take Libby's hair dryer, for example. There was—"

And Libby suddenly blushed and said, "Actually, June, that was me."

I stared at her. "*What?!*"

"It was a ridiculous idea, I know, but I—I thought that, if I was a victim of the thief, too, then maybe a certain irritating person might finally start being nice to me. So I just hid the hair dryer in my closet and pretended it'd been stolen."

Jeff burst out laughing.

"I'm glad you find this so amusing, Mr. Montague," Libby said. "I—"

"No, no, I'm not laughing at *you*, Libby, I'm—"

"Well, what's so funny, then?"

He hung his head sheepishly. "Well, there's always all this *tension* between us, you know? I figured that maybe, if you and I had both been ripped off, then we'd finally have something in common. That razor's shelf life expired a while ago, I was going to replace it, anyway...."

Libby's hazel eyes narrowed. "Are you trying to tell me you *like* me?"

"I've liked you ever since high school, Lib. But you wouldn't give me the time of day."

"You were always running with the popular crowd! I had no idea you even knew who I *was*."

"I knew who you were," he said quietly.

Oh, spare me, I thought, *they've got the* hots *for each other!*

"Well, if you *like* me," Libby said, "why did you accuse me of taking your stupid razor?"

"I didn't want to make it too obvious. And, anyway, I was all frustrated because, once Phil showed up, I thought you were all about him!"

"Oh, *that*." She giggled. "Phil and I cooked that up together, his first evening here. I explained to him that I was—*interested* in you, and he offered to help me try to make you jealous."

Jeff's brooding eyes softened. "Well, it worked. You're a hell of an actor, Phil."

"Thanks." Phil put one hand on his stomach and the other behind his back and made an awkward little bow. "I'm a little rusty. I haven't done any real performing since *I* was in high school."

"As cozy as you two have been this week," said Jeff, "I'm surprised you didn't wind *up* interested in each other."

Phil smiled. "Libby's a terrific catch, Jeff, but she's not exactly my, ah, type."

"How could she not be *anyone's* type? She's smart, she's pretty, she's—"

"She's not exactly my *gender*," Phil said delicately.

I goggled. I thought my gaydar was a hundred percent foolproof, but Phil hadn't even put a hint of a blip on my screen.

"Nuh-*uh*," I said. "You totally don't look—or act—or—"

"You've been watching too many *Will and Grace* reruns," Phil said. "In the real world, June, there's no law that says we have to look or act any different than anyone else."

I mulled that over and realized that—go figure!—he was right.

"Point taken," I acknowledged. "Okay, time out." And, pointing at each of them in turn, I summarized: "So Mrs. Smedleigh threw out Fido's bowl, Libby hid her own hair dryer, and Jeff pitched out his electric razor." My finger moved on to the next in line. "So then, who stole Moonchild's leather vest?"

The parlor was silent for a long moment, and then the aging hippie sighed and said, "Actually, man, that was me."

"No *way*," I said.

"Way. See, I had this feeling you were starting to, like, suspect me, and I decided to, like, avert suspicion by turning myself into another victim."

"Moonchild, Moonchild, Moonchild," said Dr. Le Groth indulgently, shaking his head.

"Does this mean it's cool to start wearing it again?" Moonchild said.

"You know, I'm starting to get the hang of this," I said, passing on to Miss Roberts. "So don't tell me who stole the satchel from your closet. That was *you*, right?"

Miss Roberts recoiled as if a snake had bitten her. "That is an absurd suggestion, young lady," she practically snarled. "Why on earth would any intelligent person steal from herself?"

The rest of us all looked at each other in wonderment: where had she *been* for the last ten minutes?

"But, if you didn't take it yourself," I said, "then who did?"

"Whoever took it," Miss Roberts said, "will burn in Hell! Stealing is a sin all by itself, but stealing a Bible is both a sin and a sacrilege."

And Moonchild cleared his throat uncomfortably and said, in a voice that sounded nothing at all like the aging hippie I'd come to know that week at the Roomy Toilet, "Actually, that one was me, too."

Like spectators at a tennis match, we all swiveled our heads in unison to stare at him.

"But nobody's burning in Hell for stealing a Bible," he went on. "There wasn't any Bible in that satchel, family or otherwise."

"Are you calling me a liar?" said Miss Roberts, scandalized. "And how *dare* you go into my room and steal my property!"

"I'm calling you a liar and a lot worse, ma'am."

Ma'am? Who *was* this stranger?

"But I had every legal right to go into your room, and my confiscating your satchel wasn't stealing." He reached into the back pocket of his jeans and pulled out an official-looking document. "You see, I've got a warrant."

He handed it over to her, and she gaped at it blankly.

"Let me introduce myself," he said, shaking his long, straggly hair out of his eyes. "Man, I can't wait to get a decent haircut and a shave. My real name is Forrest Copse. I'm a detective with the Walla Walla Police Department, and for the last three months I've been on undercover assignment, trailing our Miss Roberts from Washington to here. I suppose you could call it a real-life game of Copse and Roberts," he smiled wryly.

"You've been *following* her?" said Dr. Le Groth dubiously.

"Yes, sir. We were about to arrest her out in Washington when she fled the state." He tugged irritably at his beard. "I already had the long hair and whiskers—I was working a narcotics detail—so they pulled me off that assignment and sent me after her. I was on her tail, all the way across the country, and when she settled in here, I was lucky enough to be able to get the room right above hers. I've been keeping a close eye on her, gathering additional evidence, and I finally had enough to justify the search warrant for her room. I'm sorry I had to lie to you all about my identity. I hope you—"

"But what were you searching *for*?" I asked.

Before he could answer, Dr. Le Groth said, "Your real name is Forrest Copse?"

The detective shrugged. "Parents," he explained. "They thought it was clever."

"Some governor of Texas named his daughter Ima Hogg," I remembered.

"I read about that once," Libby said. "Wasn't it twin daughters, Ima Hogg and Ura Hogg?"

"No, just the one," said Forrest Copse. "The other one's urban legend. But Governor Jim Hogg was real, and he really named his only daughter Ima. Believe me, growing up with a name like mine, I heard all the stories. Crystal Shanda Lear, Ben Dover, I.P. Dailey, you name it."

"So that picture in your room," I said. "Is that really you and your mother?"

He laughed. "No, June, that's Lucy and Charlie, my wife and son."

"You're married? You're a *dad*?"

"Oh, yes. And I can't *wait* to get home. It's been way too long."

"And the sweatshirt? WWJC and some kind of soldier?"

"Warrior," he corrected. "The Walla Walla Junior College Warriors. Lucy teaches in the massotherapy program."

"Walla Walla Junior College," I repeated. "Doh."

"This is ridiculous," Miss Roberts huffed. "I don't have to sit here and listen to this nonsense."

"I'm afraid you do, ma'am. You're under arrest."

"You're arresting her?" said Mrs. Smedleigh. "But—whatever for?"

"For bank robbery," the former Moonchild said solemnly.

"Bank robbery?" Phil repeated. "Miss Roberts? You're joking!"

The detective shook his head. "She's wanted for questioning regarding six bank jobs in and around Walla Walla, and your local police are going to want to talk with her about the three here. There was over a hundred and eighty thousand dollars stashed in that satchel, and we've already matched some of the serial numbers to one of the Washington jobs and all three of the ones here."

I snapped my fingers and pointed at him. "You were listening outside her room the other night."

He nodded. "I think she was counting the take from her first local robbery. It was hard to hear, because someone in one of the other rooms was crying, but when I put my ear to her door, I could just make out the sound of paper rustling from—"

"And yesterday afternoon," I interrupted, "I saw you sitting on the sidewalk outside the Half Moon coffee shop—at the same time Miss Roberts was heading into the Mercantile Bank!"

"She was casing the place," he said. "I imagine she intended it to be her next target."

"And you were following her?"

"Exactly."

"Miss *Roberts*!" I said. "Whatever happened to 'Thou Shalt Not Steal'?"

"Why don't you just *shut up*, you brat," she snarled. "Whatever happened to 'Children should be seen and not heard'?"

"And your little *dog*, too!" Phil put in, in a perfect impression of Miss Gulch from *The Wizard of Oz*.

But I wasn't done with Forrest Copse. "Why did you—what was the word you used?—confiscate her satchel?"

"Ah, well, I wanted to throw her off balance. We already had enough to make an arrest, but I figured it'd be interesting to see how she reacted to the loss of her loot."

"And that's why she was so adamant about not wanting the police," Libby said slowly, "when she found the satchel was missing."

"The attention of the police was the *last* thing she wanted."

"But how did you get into her room?" Mrs. Smedleigh asked. "She was the one person in the house who always locked her door."

"Sorry, Mrs. S, but this—"

"You *knew* her door was locked?" I said.

She cocked her head quizzically. "Of course, dear. Who do you think changes the linens every week? Except for hers—she always collects fresh sheets and pillowcases and towels from me and takes them up herself. I'm sorry, dear, you were saying?"

"This is an old house," the detective continued, "and the locks are a joke. I waited for her to go out, then sprung the door with a credit card."

"Moonchild with a credit card," said Libby. "What a weird image."

He laughed, nodding in agreement. "I never leave home without it," he said.

"Like, wow," Jeff breathed admiringly.

And then all of a sudden I remembered something.

"Wait one second," I said.

All eyes turned to me.

"You were an actor in high school?" I said to Phil Marlowe.

His eyes lit up. "I was wondering if you'd notice that," he said. "Yes, June, as a matter of fact, I played Rolf in my school's production of *The Sound of Music*."

My mouth dropped open.

"*Lippy?*" I shouted. "Lippy Akers?"

"*Jawohl*, Fraulein Gretl," he said in a melodramatic German accent, jumping to his feet and clicking his heels together with practiced Teutonic formality.

"I *knew* I knew you from somewhere! So 'Phil Marlowe' is a phony name, too, like Moonchild?"

"Actually, no," he said. "My mom and dad were both big hardboiled-detective fans, and they named me Philip Marlowe Akers after the Chandler books. My brother Dash was only two when I was born, though, and he couldn't pronounce my first name—it kept coming out *Lippy*, and that sort of stuck until I went off to college."

"Just a second," Jeff interrupted. "Are you telling me it's not just that you making a play for Libby was an act—your whole, um, *being* here is fake?"

"Well," he said, ducking his head a bit in embarrassment, "sort of, yes. See, my parents are Sid and Sylvia Akers, of Akers & Akers Advertising, the people who make the Yummy Nibbles spots June's in. When I went off to college, the college I went off to was NYU, to study advertising, so I could eventually take over the family business. Actually, June"—he turned to me and leaned forward and lowered his voice, as if he was divulging a secret—"my roommate freshman year was Gary Stasheff—and, when Gary decided he was through with network TV, I talked him up at home, and Sid and Sylvia wound up hiring him to direct commercials for them."

"But what are *you* doing *here*?" I demanded.

"Well, okay, it's a little complicated. About six months ago, I finally made up my mind that I don't want to go into advertising, after all. I mean, with my name, you know, I want to make *movies*, real movies, not little commercials."

"Your name?" Libby asked.

"Yeah," Phil said shyly. "You didn't notice? They insist they never even realized it when they picked it, but my name is Phil M. Akers."

"Filmmakers!" I shouted, and Fido sneezed himself awake, gave me a dirty look, and stalked out from under the coffee table and off in the direction of the kitchen.

"That's me. Anyway, Mom and Dad's contacts have helped me put together the financing for a low-budget feature. It's about these twin sisters, see, and they're professional tennis players—they're sort of based on Venus and Serena Williams, only younger—except they're also detectives, they solve mysteries, like Nancy Drew. In the script, they—"

"Philip!" Libby Justice cut him off. I noticed that she and Jeff had scootched their armchairs closer together, and they were holding hands. "Will you get to the *point?*"

Phil grimaced. "Sorry. I'm really excited about this project, and I get a little carried away. It's the first really *major* thing I—"

"Lippy!" Libby warned.

"Burn," Jeff Montague said, pumping his arm, his fist clenched.

"*Sorry,*" Phil said. "The point is, I need an actress to play the twin sisters, and I want to use a new face, not just the latest teenage pop star. I, um, it sort of came to my attention that you were living here, June. I remembered you from our school play, and of course, I knew your work in the Yummy Nibbles commercials—but *The Sound of Music* was a long time ago, and the dramatic lead in a movie is awfully different from a thirty-second dog-food spot. The easy thing to do would have been to give you a screen test, but, you know, that's what everybody in the industry does. I wanted to try something different, something unique, something that would generate some press, maybe—and it was, um, suggested to me that I move in here for a week and observe you in, ah, action."

"That's what all the scribbling was about, then?" Mrs. Smedleigh wondered.

"Yeah, I was making notes for the scriptwriter, little bits to take advantage of June's personality and build the characters."

"But then what about your watch?" I insisted. "Was it really stolen, or wasn't it? Was *that* one you, too, Moon—I mean Detective?"

Forrest Copse shook his head. "No, that was it for me, June—I just hid the hippie vest and impounded the satchel."

We all looked at Phil.

"Weeeeell," he said slowly, "it sort of *was* and it *wasn't.* My, um, confederate and I were concerned that Dr. Le Groth's missing radio and Fido's missing bowl weren't enough to get you really investigating, June, so we agreed I should add another 'theft' to the picture by hiding my watch and pretending it'd been stolen. But I wasn't thinking— I should have picked something unimportant, like the cat's bowl or the hair dryer. Nobody fretted all that much when those things went missing. When I said my expensive watch was gone, though, I should have realized someone would want to bring the police in."

"And the whole point was that you wanted to watch *June* wrestle with the supposed crimes," Libby guessed.

"Right. So I had to back off and say the watch *wasn't* stolen, after all."

"So, hang on," Jeff said, trying to fit the sequence of events together. "You mean *you* stole Dr. Le Groth's radio, Phil? To give June a crime to investigate?"

The gruff old doctor coughed apologetically. "Actually," he said, "that was me."

I gaped at him. This was getting totally out of control. "But—*why?*"

"I'll tell you in a second," he promised. "In order for the explanation to make sense, though, first I must confess that I have another confession to make."

Now what?

But before he could say anything else, Mrs. Smedleigh raised a hand like a kid in school and said, "Excuse me?"

Dr. Le Groth turned to her. "Yes, madam?"

"Did you just say you stole your own radio?" she said.

"That is correct," he said, his dark-brown eyes glittering playfully.

"So"—she hesitated a moment, then counted on her fingers as she made her way through the list—"Fido's bowl, Philip's watch, Moonchild's vest, Libby's hair dryer, Jeffrey's razor, Miss Roberts' satchel, and now your radio. Are you telling me that *nothing* was stolen— the whole week?"

"Unless you want to count the three bank robberies," said Detective

Copse.

"She means from the house," Miss Roberts muttered irritably.

This was it, then. I had something to say, and I really did *not* want to say it. It would be the easiest thing in the world just to let it go, but I knew that the only way it was ever going to get resolved was if it came out in the open—and this seemed to be the obvious time and place to make that happen.

I took a deep breath.

"Actually," I said, "there *was* at least one real theft."

"And what was *that*, Miss Knight?" the doctor prompted me.

"The Oreos," I said.

Seven pairs of eyes fastened onto me.

"The Oreos?" Mrs. Smedleigh repeated, puzzled.

I nodded. "The Oreos."

"*What* Oreos?"

"At first, I thought it was Moonchild who'd taken them—but it *wasn't* you, Detective, was it?"

"I don't know what you're talking about, June."

"I know." I turned away from him. "Do you want to tell them," I asked the one pair of eyes that looked frightened, not confused, "or should I?"

Libby Justice opened her mouth to speak, but no words came out.

"Libby?" Jeff said tentatively. "What's she talking about?"

"I have no idea," she said, her gaze fixed unwaveringly on me.

"Oh, I think you do," I said. "The late-night trips to the kitchen, the missing Oreos, the lotion, the bloodshot eyes, the crying—"

"Crying?" said Jeff. "Libby, honey, have you been crying?"

"Remember, a few minutes ago, Forry said he heard crying the other night when he was listening outside Miss Roberts' door? Well, I'd followed Moonchild down to the second floor, and I heard it, too. From where I was hiding in the stairwell, I couldn't tell for sure where it was coming from, but he was listening at Miss Roberts' door, so I figured it had to be her. But it *wasn't* Miss Roberts, after all. It was you, Libby, across the hall."

She stubbornly shook her head no, but a single tear fell from her eye and betrayed her.

"Libby, what is it?" said Jeff. "What's the matter?"

"Nothing, now," she said, gazing up at him and squeezing his hand tightly.

"But something's been the matter all this week," I said. "At least that long, maybe longer."

A moment passed, and then, at last, she seemed to come to a decision. "Longer," she said, her voice so low I had to strain to hear her. "A lot longer."

"We're your friends, Libby," I assured her. "It's nothing to be ashamed of."

Once she decided to tell us, the story came out in a rush. She had wrestled with an eating disorder during her freshman and sophomore years of college, she said, binging late at night in her dorm room, then purging in a stall in the common bathroom. After hiding the problem for two years, she'd finally started seeing a counselor, and with months of therapy, she'd gotten control of her behavior and her emotions. She was still obsessive about exercise and her weight, she acknowledged, but the binging and purging were gone.

Until this week, at least. Suddenly, the stress of pitting Phil against Jeff for her attention, combined with the first of the thefts, tipped her off the balance she'd so carefully maintained since college. On Monday night, when I found her in the kitchen, she'd gone down there to eat whatever she could find. When I surprised her, though, she pretended all she wanted was a glass of milk and went back up to her room. She stole the Oreos during the day on Tuesday—right after her run, when Moonchild and I were on the porch and everyone else was still in bed—but didn't eat them, still fighting to stay in control. Finally, yesterday afternoon, she lost the battle, ate the Oreos, then went into the bathroom and stuck her finger down her throat. After she threw up, though, there was a distinctive sour smell in the bathroom, and she was frantic. She had to do something, or her secret would be discovered. So she 'accidentally' spilled the bottle of lotion to mask the odor.

"It's a sickness," she whispered. "You have no idea how horrible it is!"

Jeff put his arm around her shoulder and pulled her close, wiping tears from her cheek with his free hand.

And then she sat up straight—and, totally unexpectedly, she smiled.

"I beat this before," she said slowly, confidently. "I can beat it again."

"We know you can," Jeff said proudly. "*I* know you can."

For a little while, we all just sat there in silence. Even Miss Roberts seemed impressed by Libby's determination.

And then I remembered.

"Dr. Le Groth," I said. "You said you had *another* confession to make?"

The doctor nodded somberly. "I did. A short while ago, Phil mentioned that he had a confederate here in the house."

And he reached up and pinched his left eyeball gently between his thumb and forefinger and plucked it out of its socket, then the right one.

Well, not his *eyeballs*, of course, but the tinted brown contacts none of us had ever realized he was wearing. Underneath them, his real eyes were a deep, twinkling blue.

And then he tugged at his luxuriant head of snow-white hair—and it came away in his hands! Beneath the wig, his head was completely bald.

"Well," he said, ripping off his bushy walrus mustache with a sound like a Velcro wallet tearing open and peeling a pair of foam-rubber prosthetics from inside his cheeks, "that was me, Chickie."

"Morty?" I gasped.

"Morton?" said a stunned Mrs. Smedleigh.

I turned to her and blinked. "You know Morty the Agent?" I said, my head spinning.

"I do not," she said firmly. "But I know Morton Smedleigh, my good-for-nothing second husband!"

"Good for *something*, efter all!" Morty crowed.

The way he explained it, my temporary residence at the Roomy Toilet had been Morty's master plan from the very beginning. He knew from his dealings with Sid and Sylvia Akers that their son was interested in becoming a Hollywood producer. He knew that Lippy was looking for a star for his upcoming first film. He recommended me and urged Lippy to give me a screen test, but Lippy didn't think that would give him enough to go on and wanted to try something different. So Morty came up with the idea of a sort of 'reality test' instead.

"A *reality* test?"

"You got something wrong with your hearing, Chickie? You need a Q-Tip, maybe, to clean the wax out of your ears?"

"There's no such *thing* as a reality test," I frowned.

"There is now, dolling. I made it up. Think of it like *Who Wants to Be an Idol?* and *American Millionaire*, only without the cameras."

So Morty sold me and my parents on the idea of the emancipation stunt, and then, once the court date had been set, he got Gillian, the Akers & Akers makeup girl, to help him work up his Dr. Le Groth disguise and moved back into Mrs. Smedleigh's boarding house.

"You even wound up in your old room, Morton," the landlady smiled.

Morty leaned across the coffee table and patted her hand. "I felt right at home," he said.

"How did you know I was still here, still renting out rooms?"

He sighed. "You know, *I* never wanted the divorce, dolling. That was *your* idea."

"You've been checking up on me, all these years?"

He nodded wistfully.

Oh, spare me, I thought, they've *got the hots for each other, too!*

"Was that why you came back?" I asked. "So you could be closer to your ex-wife?"

"Well, I'll admit that was a wonderful bonus, Chickie, but mainly I moved back in to keep your parents from moidering me."

"From—"

"You're only fourteen—you think they would have agreed to let you go off and live all by your lonesome, without me to look efter you?"

I stared at him. "Morty, are you saying my parents *knew* that you were living here, masquerading as Dr. Le Groth?"

"Of *course*, that's what I'm *telling* you! I was here to keep an eye on you." He shook his head. "Oy, it feels good to get those hunks of plestic out of my eyeballs! How can ordinary people *stand* those things?"

"But you *weren't* here, not all the time."

"*An* eye, Chickie, not both eyes and a nostril. Don't forget, I got a business to run. And, anyway, if I'd been around *all* the time, I was worried you might have eventually reckanized me."

I looked him up and down. "I don't think I would have. You looked so different and sounded so, so—*not Jewish.*"

"What, Nicole Kidman from Kangaroonia is allowed to sound like a 'normal' American, and I'm not? It's called *ecting*, Chickie. You should pay attention. Who knows?" He threw Phil a wink. "Maybe someday you'll get the chance to try it."

"*This* is what you really sound like?" said Libby wonderingly.

"You think *this* is good," Morty bragged, "you should hear my Miracle Max, eh, Chickie? It's even better than my Simeon Le Groth, MD."

"Where in the world did that name come from?" I asked.

"Ah, the name. It's an anagram, dolling." He leaned forward and spilled the plastic Boggle cubes from their black tray to the coffee table. After a minute of shuffling, he'd arranged fifteen of the sixteen cubes to spell SIMEON LE GROTH MD.

"Go ahead," he said, waving a hand invitingly.

I hunkered in closer to the table and studied the cubes, then quickly reshuffled the letters into MORTON SMEDLEIGH.

"That—is—awesome," I said. "Morty, you are too much."

"Eckshally, I liked this one better," he said, moving the letters around again, this time to spell MOTHER SINGLEDOM, "but *that* good an ector, I'm not."

Mrs. Smedleigh cleared her throat delicately. "But how did you know that June would wind up here, Morton?"

"What are you talking? I *sent* her here! Efter the judge announced his decision, I gave her a note steering her to Smedley Street, and this is the only house on the block with rooms to let."

"It's a good thing I had to go to the bathroom!"

"I beg your pardon?" said Miss Roberts coldly.

So I explained about Dylan and Carson and the ROOMY TOILET sign. "But the last empty room was a hundred and fifty dollars a week, and you only gave me a hundred bucks!"

"I wanted *that* room kept available for Phil, and I knew about *this* lady's heart." He wasn't patting her hand anymore, I noticed: he was holding it firmly in both of his big paws. "I figgered she'd let you have that attic room for less."

"You always *did* know me better than anyone else, Morton," said Mrs. S.

"Only I wasn't expecting those little *pishers* to monkey with your sign. Anyway, it all worked out fine and my little starlet moved in, so I called Phil and got him over here, and it was time for the curtain to go up!"

"So you stole your own radio," Jeff said slowly, "to give June a crime to investigate."

"You got it!"

"You mean, that first night at dinner," Forrest Copse said, "when June asked you to explain about Moonchild's PTSD and you said she was too young, the truth was that you just didn't *know*?"

"I'm not really a doctor," he admitted. "I just play one on Smedley Street."

And then I remembered something else.

"What were you hiding under your pillow the other night, when I came to your room?"

"Ah," he said. "Now that's an interesting question. Think, Chickie, what were you doing right before you knocked on my door?"

I thought back. "I was on the phone," I said. "I got a call from"—my eyes widened—"from you, from Morty the Agent, telling me I had a commercial shoot set up for the next day!"

"Det's right! So when my door swung open and I saw you standing there, I—"

"—you hid your cell phone under your pillow, so I wouldn't put two and two together and realize that Simeon Le Groth and Morty the Agent were the same person!"

"Exectly!"

"And when Phil snuck into your room late Sunday night?"

"A little strategy session," Morty admitted. "I wanted to know why Phil had swiped something as silly as Fido's bowl, and he wanted to know why *I* had."

"When we realized that neither *one* of us had," Phil picked up the story, "we figured it'd just been misplaced and would turn up again, somewhere along the line."

"But we weren't sure we'd done enough to get you going with an investigation yet," Morty continued, "so—"

"Oh, I was going," I said. "It was go time for me from the minute 'Dr. Le Groth' accused me of taking his radio."

"Accused?" Morty protested. "That's a little harsh, no?"

"It felt like an accusation to *me*," I said.

"Anyway," Phil went on, "we agreed that there had to be another theft, and this time, we decided it ought to be something bigger, more valuable. We settled on my watch—"

"—but neither one of us mesterminds stopped to think that a stolen Rolex would make one of you want to call in the police."

"We're not exactly geniuses when it comes to crime," said Phil.

"You wanted a genius," Jeff grinned, "you should have gone to Ma Barker here."

"Oh, just shut up," Miss Roberts snapped.

"Hey, man," Detective Copse said, lapsing back into his Moonchild voice, "that's not cool."

And, finally, I couldn't wait another minute. "What about the movie?" I demanded. "Do I get the part?"

"*Do* you? June, when you explained about Libby—about Libby's problem, that was *exactly* the combination of intelligence and compassion I'm looking for." Phil chewed nervously on his lower lip for a moment. "Remember, this is a low-budget picture," he said. "I can't afford to pay the kind of salary a Millie Bobby Brown gets, but, if you'll do it for, say, two hundred grand, the part is yours."

I could feel my eyeballs double in size. "Two," I said. "Two—two hundred—"

"She'll take it," Morty said.

"Isn't that a decision for June to make?" asked Libby.

"Not exectly," Morty said. "Making career decisions is what she pays *me* for."

"Still—"

"I'll take it!" I shouted.

"You know, Morty," said Phil, "I've always meant to ask you how you got into the agent racket in the first place."

"Ah, well. My wife was right about me," Morty explained. "My get-rich-quick schemes never made me a nickel, so, when she kicked me out, I decided to turn over a new leaf. I was always interested in ecting, but I didn't think I had what it takes to make it as an ector. Instead, I started up as an agent, and somehow, that was the perfect fit for me. I've been getting rich slowly ever since."

"Morton," said Mrs. Smedleigh, "why didn't you ever call me, all these years?"

"You threw me out, Prunella. But everything I've done, I've done to impress you, and—"

"I'm impressed," the landlady smiled shyly. "I'm very impressed."

"Then I can finally esk you: Prunella, will you marry me again?"

Mrs. Smedleigh jumped out of her chair with a scream of delight, rushed around behind Libby, Jeff, Detective Copse, Miss Roberts, and Phil and plopped herself down on Morty's lap. "Of *course* I will, you wonderful man!" she cried and wrapped her arms around him in a tight embrace.

"Will you take his last name?" Jeff asked.

"She's already *got* my last name!" Morty laughed.

"I'll take it again," said Mrs. Smedleigh.

"Prunella Smedleigh-Smedleigh," Libby said. "It's got a nice ring to it!"

"Prunella Smeddlea Smedlee Smedleigh-Smedleigh," Mrs. Smedleigh recited. "Of Smedley Street!"

"Speaking of rings," said Morty, "I couldn't afford to give you one the last time, dolling, but now?" He reached into his pocket again. "How about putting this one on your finger?"

Mrs. Smedleigh squealed with delight. "A *diamond*! Oh, Morton, it's *gorgeous*!"

"Not heff as gorgeous as you are, Pruney."

"Pruney," Miss Roberts repeated sourly. "That is a dis*gus*ting nick-name."

"That'll be enough out of *you*," said Forrest Copse.

"And that ring is completely ostentatious," the spinster went on, as if the undercover policeman hadn't spoken. "I wouldn't be caught dead in it."

"Maybe you'll prefer *this* lovely piece of jewelry," the former Moonchild said, and slapped a chunky silver bracelet around her right wrist, then clicked the other handcuff around his own left wrist.

"Hey, speaking of names," I said, "when we were trying to figure out what Miss Roberts' first name was on Monday, you must have known all along, right, Moon—I mean Detective?"

"I liked it when you called me Forry," he said—and it still seemed weird to hear a normal grownup voice coming out of Moonchild's face.

"You're the one who suggested we check her lease!" remembered Libby.

"If it's Julia," I said, "I'll die."

"Don't die. It's not Julia."

"I absolutely forbid you to tell them," Miss Roberts snapped.

Forry chuckled. "Like you're in a position to tell me what to do, my little angel?"

"Angel?" I said, not believing it. "Her name is *Angel*?"

"Well, not exactly. It's Angelique."

Mrs. Smedleigh looked up. "Angelique?"

But we beat her to it. As if we'd rehearsed it all evening, Libby, Jeff, Phil, Morty, and I all chorused, "That's French!"

"Two hundred thousand dollars," I said slowly, trying to wrap my mind around the idea of that much money.

Morty grinned. "Thet reminds me, Chickie, I promised you some cash today. Is another hundred bucks enough to keep you going?" He reached into his pocket and pulled out another thin sheaf of twenties.

I looked at the money, looked at Morty, looked at Mrs. Smedleigh, looked back at the money. A hundred dollars was *exactly* enough to pay my second week's rent at the Roomy Toilet. But I was *done* with living on my own, I realized, at least for now.

"I want to go home," I said. "I want to tell Mom and Pops about the movie, and—Morty, I'm sick of being emancipated!"

"About that," he said. He leaned towards me and patted my cheek gently. "Technically, Chickie, you never eckshally *were* emancipated in the first place."

"What?"

"The whole situation was a setup, dolling. I wanted Phil should get a look at you as an independent young lady, so I figured the best way to do that was to—"

"You tricked me?" I shouted. "You tricked my Mom and Pops?"

"What are you, on drugs? *You,* I tricked. I admit it. But you think I could have conned your parents into a cockamamie scheme like this? They were in on it from the beginning, dolling. From *before* the beginning!"

"But, Morty, wasn't it illegal, faking out the judge like that?"

He looked at the ceiling and shook his head. "You're hopeless, Chickie. You think Justice Iz Blynde is blind? He's an old pal of mine, he owed me a favor—we set it all up together."

The lightbulb finally switched on above my head. "And that's why there were never any reporters," I said. "Because there was never anything *real* to report!"

"Not until now," said Phil M. Akers. "With your new movie career, June, you'll get all the publicity you could possibly want!"

"I—I—"

I was completely speechless. The whole thing had been a hoax, all along.

All except—

"How can I go home?" I said. "I signed a three-month lease with Mrs. Smedleigh!"

"Lease schmease," Morty scoffed. "You're fourteen years old. Nothing you sign is worth a nickel."

Mrs. Smedleigh, her head resting on Morty's shoulder, fondly said, "I wouldn't hold you to that silly piece of paper anyway, dear—now that you've brought my darling husband back to me! I'll rip it up, and you may return to your family with my blessings. You'll come and visit us, won't you?"

"And us?" Libby said, snuggling even closer to Jeff.

"Of course," I said. "All the time. I—hey, wait a minute!"

Everyone looked at me expectantly.

"What about Bennington!"

"Bennington?" Phil said, mystified. "Who's Bennington?"

"My bear! When I woke up this morning, he was missing! Somebody—"

"You never mentioned that, June."

"I thought—"

Miss Roberts made an impatient noise. "Did you look under your bed, you ridiculous child?"

I glared at her. "Under my bed? Of *course* I—"

Hold it one second. *Had* I looked under the bed?

Um, in all the excitement, maybe not.

Without another word, I stormed up the two flights of carpeted stairs and the third uncarpeted flight to the attic, threw open the door, marched across my room, fell to my knees, and looked under the bed— and there, sure enough, was Bennington, my bear, lying peacefully on his side.

I hauled him out from his hiding place and hugged him fiercely.

"You'll never guess what happened," I told him. "We're gonna be a movie star!"

Epilogue: May 31 (One Year Later)

Morty and Mrs. Smedleigh got remarried in front of Morty's old pal Judge Blynde on the morning of September 13th, the twenty-fifth anniversary of their original wedding. Mrs. S was a beautiful bride. It was a small, private ceremony, but Libby and Jeff and Phil Akers and I were all in attendance—even Fido was there, although I had to hold onto him to keep him from clawing Mrs. Smedleigh's gown to tatters.

Forrest "Moonchild" Copse and his wife Lucy had planned to fly in for the occasion, too. They had to cancel, though, at the last minute: Miss Roberts' trial was running longer than expected out in Walla Walla, and he needed to be there to testify against her. She wound up sentenced to five years in a medium-security penitentiary, and Forry says she'll probably be out in about three—but the minute they set her free, she'll be extradited back here to stand trial for her three local bank jobs.

Four hours after the Smedleighs retied the knot, Jeff and Libby had a lovely church service less than a mile from the courthouse. Libby's kid sister Becca was the maid of honor, but I got to be a bridesmaid, and I looked pretty awesome in my yellow satin dress, if I say so myself.

That evening, there was a giant double reception for both couples inside the Akers & Akers fire station. The studio had been converted into a fairyland of twinkling lights, the band was spectacular, and I got to drink *three* full glasses of champagne (much tastier than beer) and slow dance with Lippy!

At ten o'clock, the happy couples gathered on the dais to cut their wedding cake—a fabulous four-tiered affair with pink and purple rosettes accenting all four layers and two little white-gowned brides and two little tuxedoed grooms at the top.

On closer examination, the plastic figures seemed awfully realistic to me, and I tugged on Jeff's sleeve and whispered, "Did you—?"

He grinned and threw me an exaggerated wink, and I wondered how many hours' work they'd taken him.

Libby served normal human-sized slices to Morty and Mrs. Smedleigh and Jeff, and then cut a double portion for herself.

As she dug into it with her fork and lifted the first bite to her mouth, I pushed through the crowd to her side. "Libby," I whispered fiercely, "don't you think you ought to have a smaller slice?"

She leaned over and kissed my cheek. "Not tonight, honey," she said, her smile absolutely dazzling. "Tonight, I'm celebrating!"

"But what about—?"

She put her lips right up against my ear and said, "You're an angel to think about it, but I'm fine. I promise you, honey: thanks to you and Jeff and the rest of my friends at the Roomy Toilet, I am absolutely fine."

I watched her down the whole piece of cake, and kept my eye on her the rest of the evening, but she never did break for the bathroom, not once.

And me? I had *two* slices, and, let me tell you, that cake was one yummy nibble!

The next day, Morty and Mrs. Smedleigh took off for their long-delayed honeymoon—and I don't really need to tell you where they went, do I? (I'll give you a hint. They sent me a postcard with a picture of the Eiffel Tower on one side and, on the other, my name and address and the message: "Oooh, la la!")

By the end of the year, I had taken off, too—for Hollywood.

Making the movie was a lot of fun, but it was more challenging than selling dog food, I can tell you that much! And when we all gathered together in a projection room after a day's shooting to watch the rushes, and I saw two of me interacting through the magic of green-screen photography, it almost felt like I was looking at a series of stereopticon slides showing two slightly different versions of the identical image.

Phil Akers talked his old college roommate Gary Stasheff into giving the Big Time another chance and directing the picture, and Gary made the switch from videotape to film as easily as I switched from CDs to MP3s when I got my iPhone.

Allie and Brenna were afraid I'd go all star-struck and forget about them the minute I got to California, but I emailed them every day and talked with them on the phone at least twice a week. And one time in Beverly Hills when I bumped into Isabela Merced outside Nate 'n Al's deli, I made sure to get *three* autographs, one for each of us.

Near the end of the shoot, Phil flew Mom and Pops out to visit me. He paid all their expenses, and, trust me, he didn't skimp. He put them up at the Beverly Hills Hotel, rented them a limo and driver, sent them off to Disneyland—I mean, he treated them like total royalty. One evening, after we'd wrapped for the day, he took us to 6247 Hollywood Boulevard, just a few steps from the famous intersection of Hollywood and Vine, and pointed at the sidewalk. And there it was, between Gary Cooper and Sammy Davis, Jr.—inlaid into the middle of a five-pointed star was a golden silhouette of an old-time movie camera and, below that, the name June Knight.

"Someday, Juneau," my Pops said proudly, "they'll need another one like this on the Walk of Fame—for you."

I don't really like to admit this, but I cried a little then, and Mom and Pops wrapped me up in a hug that felt exactly like home.

The first time they came to the set, May 31, we were filming the climactic final sequence, as Neptune and Tranquility Wilson face each other in the women's finals at Wimbledon and Tranquility smashes a backhand into the stands. For a moment, everybody thinks she's throwing the match to let her sister, who's always below her in the international rankings, win a major tournament for a change. But her "wild" shot knocks the murderer unconscious at the *exact* moment he's about to pull the trigger and kill the line ump, so she saves the day—and comes back to win the match on the next volley.

We weren't really in England, of course, but the film crew set up an exact replica of Wimbledon's famous Center Court on a Hollywood back lot.

And, that evening, Morty called me from home. Phil had been so impressed with his performance as Simeon Le Groth that he'd offered him a part in the picture—he'd even played with the Boggle cubes and had a character named Merlen Goodsmith written into the script—but Morty was too busy being a husband and managing my newly revivified career to leave the Roomy Toilet. (At least he was getting some help with the lawn—from Dylan and Carson, of all people, who'd joined the Cub Scouts when Carson turned seven and converted from neighborhood terrors into Good Samaritans!)

"You'll never guess, Chickie!" his voice boomed across the miles. "You won't even believe me when I tell you!"

"Tell me what?"

"Today's *Straight Shooter*, dolling. The front-page headline, letters a foot and a half high, practically: 'Fifteen-Year-Old Ectress Takes Parents to Court.' Did I tell you, Chickie, or what?"

"You told me '*Fourteen*-Year-Old Actress,'" I reminded him. "And I took Mom and Pops to *Center* Court, not *court*. That's not exactly the same thing."

"So I was a little off," Morty acknowledged. "So sue me!"

About the Author

Josh Pachter's short crime stories have been appearing in *Ellery Queen's Mystery Magazine* and many other places since the late 1960s. He has edited more than a dozen anthologies, including Anthony Award-nominated *The Beat of Black Wings: Crime Fiction Inspired by the Songs of Joni Mitchell* (Untreed Reads), *Paranoia Blues: Crime Fiction Inspired by the Songs of Paul Simon* (Down and Out Books), and *Happiness Is a Warm Gun: Crime Fiction Inspired by the Songs of the Beatles* (Down and Out Books); and *EQMM*'s "Passport to Crime" department regularly features his translations of stories by Dutch and Flemish authors. His first novel, *Dutch Threat,* was published by Genius Books in 2023 and nominated for the Agatha, Lefty, and Macavity awards. *First Week Free at the Roomy Toilet* is his first book for younger readers. In 2020, the Short Mystery Fiction Society selected him to receive its Golden Derringer Award for Lifetime Achievement.

SOCIAL MEDIA HANDLES: Facebook (josh.pachter)

AUTHOR WEBSITE: www.joshpachter.com

Also by Josh Pachter

For a complete list of published short stories, visit
http://www.joshpachter.com/bib/bibliography.html

BOOKS

First Week Free at the Roomy Toilet, by Josh Pachter (Level Best Books, 2024)

Friend of the Devil: Crime Fiction Inspired by the Songs of the Grateful Dead, edited by Josh Pachter (Down and Out Books, 2024)

Happiness Is a Warm Gun: Crime Fiction Inspired by the Songs of the Beatles, edited by Josh Pachter (Down and Out Books, 2023)

Dutch Threat, by Josh Pachter (Genius Book Publishing, 2023)

Paranoia Blues: Crime Fiction Inspired by the Songs of Paul Simon, edited by Josh Pachter (Down and Out Books, 2022)

The Adventures of the Puzzle Club, by Ellery Queen and Josh Pachter (Crippen & Landru, 2022)

The Man Who Solved Mysteries: More Short Fiction by William Brittain, edited by Josh Pachter (Crippen & Landru, 2022)

Monkey Business: Crime Fiction Inspired by the Films of the Marx Brothers, edited by Josh Pachter (Untreed Reads, 2021)

Only the Good Die Young: Crime Fiction Inspired by the Songs of Billy Joel, edited by Josh Pachter (Untreed Reads, 2021)

The Great Filling Station Holdup: Crime Fiction Inspired by the Songs of Jimmy Buffett, edited by Josh Pachter (Down & Out Books, 2021)

The Further Misadventures of Ellery Queen, edited by Josh Pachter and Dale C. Andrews (Wildside Press, 2020)

The Misadventures of Nero Wolfe, edited by Josh Pachter (Mysterious Press, 2020)

The Beat of Black Wings: Crime Fiction Inspired by the Songs of Joni Mitchell, edited by Josh Pachter (Untreed Reads, 2020)

Amsterdam Noir, edited by Rene Appel and Josh Pachter (Ambo|Anthos, 2018; Akashic Books, 2019)

The Man Who Read Mysteries: The Short Fiction of William Brittain, edited by Josh Pachter (Crippen & Landru, 2018)

The Misadventures of Ellery Queen, edited by Josh Pachter and Dale C. Andrews (Wildside Press, 2018)

The Tree of Life, by Josh Pachter (Wildside Press, 2015)

The Mahboob Chaudri Mystery Megapack, by Josh Pachter (Wildside Press, 2015)